BLACK
WOMB

MATTHEW LEDREW

BLACK WOMB

CORAL BEACH CASEPILES

Published in Canada by Engen Books, Chapel Arm, NL.

Library and Archives Canada Cataloguing in Publication data is available on the publisher's website.

Distributed by:
Engen Books
www.engenbooks.com
submissions@engenbooks.com

First mass market paperback printing: October 2010
Second edition mass market paperback printing: October 2012
Third edition mass market paperback printing: February 2019

Cover Image: Shutterstock

For
Ellen

PROLOGUE
SHE RAN

She turned around fast, too afraid to blink.

She was running so fast that great clumps of her knotted black hair swung into her eyes while she searched the snow covered hillside desperately, brief breaks in the cloud cover providing her with enough visibility to make out movement in the dense forest behind her.

Breath escaped her mouth in great white puffs, swirling around her head like cigarette smoke. Her eyes darted across the waving white horizon of the small clearing she had just sprinted across. Panting loudly, she tried to hear above the sound of her breath and the snow crunching beneath her bare feet, now blue and numb from hours of constant running.

She tried to wiggle her toes but the exertion on her frozen extremities sent bolts of electric pain up her legs and into her spine, finally exploding out the back of her head. She decided not to do it again.

She took one last heave as she leaned against a large oak tree next to her. Her back muscles tensed even more for a moment, then finally loosened for the first time in hours. She closed her eyes only briefly. They stung fiercely from the dry cold and days without sleep. Adjusting the large bulge of blankets she had stuffed under her shirt for warmth, she placed one arm firmly beneath them and huddled them close to her breasts.

A sound in front of her made her eyes snap open once again, her large pupils instantly scanning the landscape relentlessly. There was no wind, and the thick patches of evergreen trees scattered throughout the clearing hung as lifelessly as if they were in a painting. Their heavy branches were weighed down by the snow, making them droop and resemble old sagging faces. They glared at her like gargoyles, each one of them screaming, scowling, laughing and passing judgment on her with their collective brows turned downward in horrible sneers of distaste.

Every movement of the branches, every rustling of a shrub, became a possible danger. Became the idea that something could be there, looking back across the field for any sign of movement, just as she was.

She held her breath until her chest ached even more, her heart rate climbing. Her veins felt like they were on fire, a stark contrast to her skin, which was now turning blue from the intense cold. She knew it had been a bad idea to stop moving, but she had to.

An owl let go of the branch a few feet above her, not making a sound. The snow loosened from the dead branch and fell to the ground, becoming invisible once there. The great bird circled a small area around her before flying silently off to the south and deeper into the woods, where she had been heading.

She chuckled to herself softly, shaking her head at her own paranoia. She had not only doubled, but tripled back upon herself more than once. She had purposely walked in three large circles every mile since she had started running, hours ago. The only thing she had not done was cover her tracks, a near impossibility when wading through three feet of snow.

Keeping a suspicious eye on the open slope before her, she began to examine herself. The black parka she had stolen was still in relatively good condition. It had only been ripped once or twice at the elbows by stray tree limbs. The brown fox fur that lined the neck was still completely intact and had managed to keep her upper body at least a little warm. That kept her heart and lungs warm and kept them pumping warm blood and air through her body, giving them the strength and vitality they would not have had otherwise. Below the waist was only the bottom half of a simple nightdress and a normal paper hospital gown. It provided about as much protection against the cold as 'thinking warm thoughts'.

She grimaced when she noticed a large gash in her right knee, probably from when she had tripped a quarter mile back trying to create a shortcut through a thick patch of shrubs and roots. Bits of twigs and pebbles stuck out of it, along with blood that was now frozen onto the skin. She tried hard not to think about how painful that would be once she got feeling back in the lower half of her body.

She did not even look at her feet, afraid of what she might see. She was afraid that the odd snap she had heard two miles into her run had been one of her toes coming off. She did, however, take note of a viscous green fluid that had splattered all the way up to her pelvis at some point. It seemed to be fading even as she watched it, like suntan lotion as it seeped into your skin. A feeling of relief came over her and she began to think there was at least some hope for her frozen appendages.

Deciding she had wasted enough time, she pushed off from the tree with one arm, her body groaning in rebellion as she forced it into movement again. Looking at the forest ahead of her, she saw no real path in sight. It looked like a black and white etching from a Brothers Grimm story, especially the oaks with their leaves long dead from the fall. Yet as horrible as it seemed, she thought she could see the pale light of civilization past them and she dared to think that she might be close to some form of sanctuary.

She turned and smirked at the tree she had leaned against, looking at the withered knots and crannies that made up its haggard face.

Someone had told her years ago that every tree had a face. She had thought it to be fairy tale bullshit, but if tonight had proven anything it was just the opposite. They had been her only company since she'd entered the treeline.

"Thanks," she whispered humbly.

Old Man Oak seemed to approve.

Then she saw it out of the corner of her eye.

She turned, her hair again catching in her eyes, toward the soft glint she could have sworn she had seen near the edge of the clearing. It was gone now and she squinted and strained her eyes toward the spot where it had been, wishing to the moon for just a little more light.

She got her wish as a pair of headlights turned on

from the horizon, illuminating her in bright yellow. Her mouth wide, she thrust up her hands to protect herself from the temporary blindness so instinctively that she almost dropped the blankets she'd been using for warmth.

Immediately after she was doused in light, the source of the glint she had seen was identified. Rifle fire erupted all around her, turning the face of Old Man Oak into sharp splintered sticks. They bounced off her parka as she turned and bolted into the black forest with more gunshots following her, tearing up the virgin snow and sending it sailing in all directions at once.

She pumped her legs harder and faster than she ever had as sweat began to freeze to her scalp. She heard the sound of three... no, four engines revving to life as they started their decent down the clearing after her.

Sharp twigs nipped at her exposed flesh as she fled into the nearest clump of trees too dense for one of their snowmobiles to follow through. She started to make her way toward the light she had seen a moment ago, but had already lost track of.

⋀⋁⋀

The leader of the drivers vaulted off a mogul, landing in an outburst of fresh powder. It sprayed up into his face and parka. The other drivers followed in suit close behind. He leaned over the right edge of his snowmobile and took aim at the woman as her form began to disappear through the trees. He trained his eye on her while struggling to maintain his balance, a circular red lens over his right eye. It looked like a futuristic monocle and displayed information to him, feeding him decreasing statistics on her distance from him, wind resistance, and speed. Smirking to himself from beneath his gray toque, he applied first pressure to the trigger slowly. He fought to keep the barrel in line with the small of her back as she bobbed and weaved through the brush.

His left ski hit a rock hidden by the snow and made his arm jostle to the right, the gun firing at the same time. The shoulder strap on his rifle came loose and he cursed as he was forced to drop it to steady the vehicle. He watched her continue to move away from his team as one of the other drivers stopped at a line of brush to continue on foot, leaving the engine running.

The leader turned toward the front, trying to see if there was a way he could continue with his machine. All at once, it seemed like his snowmobile had stopped moving. The tree that the woman had been standing next to was much closer than he had judged it to be and was moving directly at him.

He barely got the chance to react as the front slammed into the trunk at top speed. He got the chance to think one thought, comprised of exactly one word, before the left side of his face ripped across the jagged, splintered wood of the tree. The momentum carried him forward, slamming his shoulder completely out of socket before launching him into the bushes behind it. The broken red glass from his lens protruded from multiple gouges across the right side of his face. He could already feel his mouth and lungs fill with gummy, coppery liquid and bile through the dual holes in his lungs made by fractured ribs. His spleen had been ruptured. Before he fell into unconsciousness and the certain death that would come soon afterward, he couldn't help but notice his blood. How black it looked against the pure white of the snow, when bathed in the stark moonlight.

⋀⟨⋀

She saw the light in front of her again now. It flickered on and off, this way and that, like a candle trying to hold its own against a light breeze. She pressed forward with tears streaming down her cheeks and freezing there. Blood poured from the gunshot that had just grazed her hip and now gushed down over her thigh, at least serving to keep her warm.

She could hear him behind her. He was getting closer and closer with every foot they ran, each stride of his powerful legs propelling him at least twice as far as hers were.

The blankets moved and shifted under her breasts, and again she steadied them with her hand.

The light got clearer and clearer and she began to see colours and shapes. Two, then three sources of light and finally a fourth as she cleared a large overhanging branch. Biting down hard on her lower lip, she clutched her bundle against her chest and ploughed her way through one last thicket. She emerged into a clearing on the other side and stopped dead in her tracks, kicking up powder as she did so.

It erupted out of the ground in front of her as if from nowhere. The lights of civilization were apparent now, a mile or two behind it. Its twin steeples rose high into the mist that she hadn't realized was there a moment ago. The flickering lights behind its massive stained glass windows made the images and characters on them dance vibrantly.

It was a convent.

Large wooden doors that looked too big to open were no more than four yards in front of her, their huge brass knockers begging for her to take them in her hand.

She hesitated, staring up this time at actual gargoyles grinning down at her from on high. They protected the central statue on the beautiful architectural masterpiece: the mother Mary. She cradled her child Jesus in her arms and stared down at him. She stared not as a woman who gave her son to better the world she lived in, but as a mother, looking upon her one love and greatest achievement.

She unzipped her parka slowly and carefully removed the bundle of dull green blankets held within. Taking off the top layer, she looked down upon her child, curled into a shivering ball to protect itself against the harsh cold. It was devoid of the cuts and scrapes that tattered her body, yet somehow there was blood on its still-pink skin. She realized after a moment that it was her own. The baby's skin was beginning to turn a hue of light blue despite her efforts to keep it warm, and she was relieved when its chest rose and fell before her. Tearing her gaze away from her wonderful child, she turned back toward the convent.

The gargoyles seemed to have turned toward her while she was looking away and now leaned in to stare at the child with renewed interest. Their devilish smiles and curling tongues were lashing out with thirst.

She turned her head when she heard a rustling not far behind her, snapping her out of the momentary trance the sight of the building had placed her in. She bolted forward, grabbing one of the brass knockers and slamming it three times as hard as she could.

There was no response.

Her lower lip quivering and bleeding, she looked down at the child, too cold to even open its eyes. Salt tears streaming down her face, she kissed it once on the forehead then laid it on the stone step.

The gargoyles seemed to dance and bounce with clandestine glee as she turned and ran back the way she came.

The sound of her footfalls continued for a moment or two before a shot rang out onto the chilled air, followed only by silence.

Several long moments passed. The biting winter wind began to pick up again, making the few hairs on the baby's head stand on end as it shivered and shook.

A light went on upstairs in the convent, then another, not far from the doors.

Crouched at the tree line, a dark-skinned man wearing another gray toque and parka uniform peeked through the clearing at what was taking place. He knelt down low and aimed his rifle, set the crosshairs to intersect at the child's head, and placed his finger on the trigger.

The massive front door of the building creaked open, sending a beam of light down onto the infant. It winced, raising its chubby arms to block the new brightness as it washed over him, suddenly replaced by a shadow.

Sister Ruth Main looked down at the helpless child, still squinting from the brightness. Her old sagging features went from shocked to a kind smile as she pushed either side of her habit behind her shoulders and knelt down, picking up the baby and holding it close to her warm body. The infant opened its eyes and looked at her, the light from inside streaming around her head as she smiled at it, cooing softly. She looked like an angel.

The man in the brush shifted his gun sight, making sure it still intersected with the child's head.

Ruth let her hand rest on the child's head, pushing back its soft hair until it stood on end. The golden crucifix that dangled around her neck caught the child's eye and it followed it intently, its small mouth opening in toothless awe.

He paused, slowly taking pressure away from the trigger before finally letting go of it altogether. The barrel dropped away as he watched Ruth cradle the child and look all around the grounds, before taking the babe back inside. He frowned, a determined look coming over him, then turned around and began the walk back toward his snowmobile.

January 28. Subject female, early twenties, caucasian, roughly 150 pounds. Reference number 08276. Was exposed to the darkness during first trimester of pregnancy. Subject is now twenty one days pregnant. This one appears hopeful.

February 12. Subject showing rejection to vitamins and other birth enhancing chemicals. There are an unusual number of white blood cells in the patient's blood stream. Further studies into possibilities of diabetes and other diseases' are pending. Considering Philidamide.

March 1. Subject has gone into early labor. Child appears to be perfectly healthy, with no sources of the darkness within his genetic structure. The project has been terminated, marked FAILURE.

March 7. Female subject has fled with her child. One soldier killed during said escape. Female subject was captured approximately five miles from town. As per procedure she was made insulin-deficient prior to testing. Prolonged time away from treatment center caused kidney failure and other complications resulting in her death. However, the child was too young to be altered in any such way...

HE WILL SURVIVE . . .

CHAPTER ONE
SMALL TOWN

15 YEARS LATER

"So, you going to Julian Grendel's party on Friday?" she asked him, paying little attention to his response or even if he gave one. It was one thing he almost admired about Sara Johnson; she had a way of controlling you without even letting you know you were being controlled. Maybe it was her lips, or how she subconsciously played with her curly blonde hair all the time, but she always did it. She was good at it, and she knew it.

"Uh, I'm not sure. I was thinking about hitting the Factory with Mike," Alexander Drew replied, half concentrating on her and half watching out for Grendel himself. For whatever reason, Grendel didn't like people not coming to his parties. He brushed a hand through his dark brown hair. His eyes darted about skittishly, meeting those of every person who walked past the two of them, then immediately dropped to the floor. Finally, they found her. Her perfect body, not too thin, those lush pink lips, short blonde hair and the way her blue eyes looked right through you, slicing at you.

"Oh, come on, Xander," she whined. She said his name like it was some kind of a joke.

He didn't remember the orphanage, but he remembered how he got stuck with the name Xander. Every child had been named after a saint. There were three children who had been given the name Alexander by separate caretakers. For identification purposes, one was Alexander, another was Alex, and he was just plain Xander.

He hated the name; it was just another thing to make him stand out that tiny bit when all he wanted was not to be noticed… and the one person he did want to notice him said his name as if it were a joke.

"Alright, I'll come. But you have to promise me you'll make sure Mike and Cathy don't ditch me like the last time," he reasoned, heaving a massive sigh as he gave in.

"They didn't ditch you."

He gave her a droll, tired look.

"They didn't!" she laughed, slapping his arm playfully.

He frowned, then rolled his eyes and nodded.

"Oh, come on. Don't sulk. You know I'm right. They love you."

"They do," he agreed finally. "They really do. They love me and they're there for me and they are the best of friends - except in public. In public, it's like we never met."

"Drama queen."

"Oh, I'm not saying they *try* it or anything... it's just the way things are. I get it." He forced a smile, making eye contact with her. "I don't even think they realize they do it."

She gave him a little smile, the right corner of her lip curling just enough to make her irresistible as she fixed her black tube top, even though it hadn't really needed it. In all honesty, it was not so much a tube top as it was a strip of black tape going across her chest. That was the other thing about Sara. Besides having the looks of a goddess and the voice of an angel... she dressed like the devil. Skimpy tank tops and hip-hugger jeans. Fishnet stockings wrapped around her hands and covering her forearms. Large hoop earrings, at least two rings on each finger (silver on the left and gold on the right) and all that was just one outfit.

"I promise," she said, after she had spent enough time fiddling with her attire to make him twitch. "They'll be good little boys and girls, as long as you are."

He snorted, rolled his eyes, and closed his locker door with a clang. He pulled his book bag onto his back as the two of them started walking toward the front exit of Coral Beach High, the flat-out boring high school in the mediocre town of Coral Beach, getting ready to walk home together just like they did every day.

"So, what's new today?" he asked, shooting her a smile. "Anything scandalous going on?"

Now it was his turn to know the answer before she gave it. He asked something like that of her every day, because to her there was always something scandalous happening. Everywhere. Always. But to be fair, scandalous things seemed to happen around her anyway.

"Well," she started, smirking to herself proudly. "I heard from Julie Peterson today that the reason Derek has been so on edge lately is because Theresa had to take the test."

"Yeah," Xander nodded. "That Family Living test was bad news. I think I must have only gotten an eighty-five or something..."

She turned and gave him a little slap on the arm. "Not that test, you halfwit. A pregnancy test."

Xander's eyes went wide for a moment as he held open the front door for her, which she barely acknowledged. "Oh."

"Yeah."

"Why would Derek be messed up over that?" he asked naively.

She shot him a look.

"Ah. Forget I asked."

"Done."

"Wasn't she supposed to be with Jamie?"

"They broke up."

"Why? I mean, besides the 'she may be pregnant from another man' thing?"

"That's just a rumor. The real reason was because he cheated on her," she smirked to herself coyly.

"With who?" he moaned, feeling a relationship headache coming on.

"Me," she said proudly, and he realized that this would become a migraine before it was over.

Xander finished walking home with Sara, like always. They lived next door to one another, and had since either of them could remember. Since they were children. Every day he'd remember little things like where he'd fallen out of the tree trying to sneak up to her room when they were six, when she had been sick and wanted to play. Or on his lush, green lawn where she had found out how he felt when they were twelve.

He had had a huge crush on her that summer and had been sitting on the sidewalk between their houses, burning their initials into a piece of wood. She had started toward him on roller blades and he had dropped the wood and ran into his house. She'd picked it up and looked at it, then thrown it into the trees on her way down the road, never actually speaking of it. He could still remember the scent of the wood as it burned every time he thought of it. It was the way love smelled.

At that age, most children were confident of their own immortality. That they could do anything, and go anywhere. But it was then that he realized how different he was from his friend. She was a princess in their school. Other kids wondered why she lowered herself to talking to him. He was… abnormal. Subnormal. Less than human. Those who actually took notice of him could barely stand him. But when he was around her, none of it mattered. On that ten minute walk from home to school and back again, the world could fall down around his ears and crush him every day, and he wouldn't care. He would ask for more.

"So, about the party…" Sara stared, looking up at him, her eyes sparkling.

"Yeah?" he said, his voice rising with the smallest speckle of hope.

"Jamie's going to be coming with me, so you better not get all weird with him… okay? I like him."

"Yeah, sure," he said softly, his eyes fading back downward.

She walked up her driveway and through the off-white door into her house.

He watched it for a second after she was gone as if she were still there, then walked into his own house.

He went straight up his stairs and into his room, passing by his father quickly to avoid the usual barrage of questions.

He logged onto his computer and suddenly he wasn't a loser anymore. He wasn't anybody's doormat. He was the king of everything. He was everything. The ultimate hacker.

A sly smile spread over his face as he turned on the screen, illuminating his face in bright blue in the dark room, his eyes alive with vindictive excitement as he opened up all of his programs.

$\wedge\!\langle\rangle\!\wedge$

The Factory.

A local arcade/club/dance hall where all the teens went when there was nothing else to do. Located in the scenic downtown of Coral Beach, which was roughly a five minute walk from 'up' town, the Factory jutted up from the otherwise calm landscape, always loud and exciting and neon.

Jamie Dawkins leaned over one of the many pool tables that adorned the club, raising an eyebrow as he tried to figure out his shot. His leather sports jacket crumpled and scrunched noisily every time he moved, impeding his ability to shoot. Many times he had pushed up the sleeves in an effort to alleviate the inconvenience, but they always fell back down almost immediately. But he dared not take it off. His brother had worn that jacket when he was captain of the Coral Beach Cougars, and his father before that. Now that he was finally captain, it barely ever left his back. Some even said he showered with it on.

As good as he was at football (almost undisputed as the best in the entire region), his abilities did not translate into every sport. Pool, as it turned out, was not one of them. His face began to turn red as he huffed in frustration. Standing back up and grabbing the chalk, he fumbled it over the top of his stick and smeared a little onto his hands as he had once seen some pool champ on ESPN do. Nervous and more than a little agitated, the bulky teen rubbed a hand over his close-cut hair, accidently leaving some of the blue powder there as well.

Across the table his opponent, Mike Harris, snickered a little at the sight. Mike nearly had all of the high balls sunk, but Jamie was still on his third low. It was probably a good thing that this wasn't one of the high profile tournaments that were held here once or twice a month, or Jamie would've been the laughing stock of the school for at least a week.

Mike glanced into the large, circular mirror that was mounted in the top corner of the room, watching a cute black-haired girl without her even realizing it. She had an adorable round face with rose-red lips and wore a tight top over her slim figure to match them. Her eyes were almost almond shaped, a trait accentuated by how she wore her eyeliner. She wore loose, relaxed jeans with frills going down the sides, and held her Coke near her breasts, playing with the straw a little with her tongue.

Smiling, he turned back to the game.

On the other side of the room, Cathy Kennessy sipped

on her soda subconsciously. She wasn't really paying attention to the game. She was watching Mike. Very intently. The way he moved with his large, square shoulders and tall frame. The way shocks of his blonde hair fell over his brow, touching his sky blue eyes in places. The way his freckles dotted his cheeks. And his arms, she couldn't forget his arms. Those large, muscular arms that he used to pick her up and spin her around and hold her when she was cold.

From across the room, Grendel watched Cathy from the bar, smirking to himself. He was wearing a ratty button-down shirt as a coat over his tee shirt, the sleeves of which extended well over his hands, absorbing moisture from the bar into their tattered fibers.

He took one last swig of cola from his glass, feeling it sizzle as tiny flickers of it connected with his cheeks. He took notice of the waitress as she wiped a ring of condensation from his glass away even as he picked it up, throwing her a wink. She rolled her eyes at him.

Wiping the pop from his face, he started across the room.

He popped up next to Cathy, producing a smile so large it made his ears wiggle.

"Great music, huh?" he said cheerfully, looking her up and down.

She turned to him, glancing at his large, innocent eyes for a moment. His bald head and his attempt to grow scruff along the sides of his face and chin made him look just a little silly, enough to make her laugh whenever she saw him.

She stopped for a second to acknowledge the very

music he was talking about. She had been so engrossed in watching her boyfriend that she had barely even noticed it. They were a local band called Ragnarok, playing their own rendition of *Superman's Dead* by Our Lady Peace. It was good, but not as good as the original and definitely not as good as the band's own music.

She gave Grendel a little nod.

This was how it always was. She had her outside image, she attended the games, listened to the music, put on the face. But all she really cared about was her boyfriend and her friends. Friends like Sara and Xander.

Poor Xander.

She called him that so much that some of the juniors had actually started to believe it was his name. She'd always thought he and Sara were perfect for one another, but Sara had, like, serial boyfriends. She went through them like popcorn. Cathy always warned her that she would eventually hit a kernel and get a bad one, or she'd pass over a really good one.

"So, what's going on?" Grendel asked, leaning against the counter next to her. He followed her gaze until he was watching the game as well.

"Not much," she said, an evil smirk spreading across her lips. "Mike's kicking Jamie's ass."

Grendel laughed. "What else is new? Jamie's about as good at pool as he is at football."

"That why he's captain and you didn't make the team?" she poised playfully, raising an eyebrow in his direction. She turned away from Mike for the first time since the conversation began.

"Hey, I just couldn't take the politics of the game, is

all."

"How is a bunch of testosterone crazed idiots running around and slamming into each other wearing glorified coconut shells and pouring Gatorade over each other political?"

"I see no differences between what you just said and what goes on in government." He paused. "Except football players usually have more going on for them upstairs than your average president."

Across the room, Jamie finally parted with his jacket, laying it on a hanger near him. He leaned in for his shot as Mike, Cathy and now Grendel all watched. He tried to get the seven ball in the side pocket with an easy straight shot, but the table was old and the cloth was lumpy and torn in spots. The cue missed the seven completely and ended up bouncing harmlessly off the side.

Smiling, Mike leaned in quickly (almost before the cue had stopped rolling) and finished the game with a bank shot that sunk the eight ball into the side pocket.

Jamie looked enraged, but he suppressed the anger and calmly put down the pool cue.

"Good game," he mumbled under his breath.

"Yes, it was." Mike laughed, shaking his opponent's hand curtly. "Now pay up."

Jamie sighed, then reached into his pocket and pulled out a five, grumbling as though he had expected Mike to forget.

"Wanna play again?"

"Ha," Jamie smiled. "Not likely. I think I'm just gonna head home and call Sara."

"Cool," Mike shrugged, putting his stick away and

walking over to where Cathy and Grendel stood. He placed the five down on the counter and waited for Roxanne to come around so that he could buy Cathy a snack before they left.

"You won!" she chirped happily, spreading out her arms as though she were cheering him on from the sidelines of the Superbowl.

"I did," he laughed, placing a hand on her hip. "Wait, was that in doubt? Did you have doubt-face?"

"Never once," she assured him, glancing from the five dollar bill to rack of snacks and goodies behind the bar. She knew what it meant. She'd seen it before.

He gave her a quick kiss, then extended it into a longer one.

Jamie shrugged, justifying his loss with the fact that the money would be put to good use buying Cathy and Mike dinner, but more importantly, some much needed alone time. Life was busy, even if their parents would argue that they were lazy.

He grabbed his leather Cougars jacket and waved a goodbye to Mike and Cathy, although they hardly noticed. He smirked to himself as he opened the door and walked out.

Grendel looked away from Mike and Cathy as they went deeper and deeper into their kiss. As he glanced back at them, a disgusted look coming over his face. His eyes slowly fell down her backside until he found himself looking at things he knew that he shouldn't. He turned toward the door and smiled a little. "I think I'll head out, too. You two seem like you wanna be alone."

They didn't answer, each of them too deep in the other.

He got up and walked for the door, slamming it behind him.

Neither of them noticed or cared.

Jamie started to walk down the street. It was getting
dark, and he lit up a cigarette and took a long draw. Then
he looked down at it and got suddenly revolted with himself. He'd smoked for years. He knew what it was doing
to him, why he was having trouble running the whole distance of the field now. He finished the smoke on the corner and threw the smouldering butt down onto the sidewalk, swearing to himself that he'd never touch another
one of them.

He thought he heard something behind him, then
started walking again, zipping his jacket to protect himself against the harsh cold of night. He could see his own
breath as it swirled up around his head like a wreath.

A dark figure stepped out of the shadows behind him
and stepped in time with him, squishing the discarded
cigarette beneath his heavy feet.

Jamie heard it now, he was sure of it. The footsteps
were getting closer and closer to him. He started to pick
up his pace, and so did the second set of footsteps. He
broke into an all out run, hearing the second set do the
same, close behind him. He got to the end of the block
and made a sharp turn, beads of sweat already forming
on his forehead. He got to the end of the next block and
bent over from the pain in his side. He shouldn't have gotten such a painful stitch already. He ran three times this
far on the football field every day. Yet his lungs heaved,

each breath brought agony, and he made a small grunt from the pain. He looked up, turning around to face his attacker for the first time.

There was nobody there. He searched the streets and doorways around him with his eyes, seeing nothing.

Suddenly, he started to laugh.

He stomped his foot down onto the black pavement, listening to the echo of the sound returning to him. He'd been running from noises, shadows. He laughed once more at his own stupidity.

"You're losing it," he whispered to himself softly.

He turned the corner and immediately bumped into a large, dark figure. The person was covered by a coat that seemed to be made out of shadows, with eyes burning bright with hatred as it moved toward him menacingly.

Jamie screamed loudly and took off in the other direction, but his stitch got the better of him again, this time right away. The shadow-figure grabbed him, and pulled him into the darkness. A dagger appeared from his coat and jabbed into Jamie's right side.

Blood gushed from the treads etched into the sides of the blade, splattering onto the street with a sickening splashing sound.

As Jamie's vision became hazy and he realized it was over, he stopped struggling against his killer's iron grip. He fell to the ground, and the last thoughts to run through his head were that maybe if he had given up smoking just a little earlier, he might have been able to run just that little bit further...

Xander woke up at his computer, his hair a tattered mess.

He fell asleep on the keyboard like that often, staying online to the point past exhaustion. He wiped a bit of drool from his chin. His skin felt sticky and wet, like he had just gotten out of a bath of honey. He touched himself, and found that his flesh was clammy and warm. Glancing up at his screen, he noticed he had mail. **Babygurl@first-timebreak.com**. That was Sara's e-mail.

He opened it and scrolled down through the prattle that headed most of her e-mails, more gossip about Theresa and Derek, along with a few other tidbits about who Julie and Tommy were dating now... Then he noticed a little sentence at the end.

Do you know where Jamie is? He was supposed to call me...

At the mention of Jamie Dawkins, Xander's nostrils flared. He closed and deleted the e-mail, then logged back onto his usual chat page, rubbing his tired eyes. He felt as though he hadn't gotten any sleep at all.

He hated all of Sara's (what was it Cathy had called them?) serial boyfriends. Sometimes he really just wished that all the Jamie Dawkins of the world would just drop dead.

Suddenly, he heard the familiar chime as someone online contacted him.

Hello Pinkerton, came the instant message. Xander looked at it and smirked. He hadn't been called that in real life in years, but it had always made for an entertaining screen name.

Oh. Hi soul. How's life? he replied, typing quickly.

Alright. I've been looking at something weird online. I discovered some kind of bizarre... thing. I don't have a password decoder as sophisticated as you do, I thought you might wanna take a look at it.

Sure. What's the site?

Something called engen.com. Oops. Gtg!

'got to go'?, Why?

But he was gone, just as quickly as he had come online. Xander frowned. Soul had always specialized in finding weird stuff online. Weird government conspiracy videos, proof that the Moon landing was faked, the Paris Hilton video... This was probably nothing, but still, it was worth checking out.

But it would have to wait until morning.

He let out a long yawn, then got up and walked the two feet to his bed, fell onto his mattress, and slept.

Officer Tom Lensherr of the Coral Beach police precinct wasn't used to weird stuff.

That's partly why he joined the force of this town. He had always said that nothing ever happened in Coral Beach. And by nothing he didn't mean nothing bad. Literally *nothing* ever occurred here. It was as if this town's purpose was solely to exist.

Lensherr never much cared for gore either. He hadn't seen a real dead body since his first day on the job a few months ago, and that had only been a heart attack victim.

So what he saw as he shone his flashlight into the darkened alley made his stomach turn. The image was permanently burned into his mind, enough so that he would spend the remainder of his days curling into his wife for comfort every night as he cried himself to sleep.

Jamie Dawkins was sprawled out on the ground in a dark alley, thrown down like a piece of trash. There was blood all around him, smeared onto the brick walls that must have been the last thing he saw. His torso had been cut open revealing the inner body cavity and places where organs should have been, but weren't. His skull had been bashed in, and looked like it had been done over and over again.

There was a yellow, gloppy substance all around him, something that Lensherr recognized as intestines from a report he'd seen on the Discovery Channel a few weeks ago. The distinct aroma of dung and blood assaulted his senses, making him gasp for air that only brought more of the foul odor. Flecks of marrow and bone checkered the ground around them, and the boy's empty eye sockets glared at him, screaming at him, his broken nose and shattered teeth turning his face into one bloody maw.

Lensherr nearly vomited before picking up his radio and calling for reinforcements from the morgue. Then he shone his flashlight onto the blood blurred walls and saw what the blood spelled: **Black Womb**.

CHAPTER TWO
CADAVER

"Did you hear about what happened to Jamie Dawkins?"

The news spread through the school like wildfire. Within moments of opening its doors, it seemed as if everyone in school knew. It was the hushed topic on everyone's lips, in every gaze, in every movement. It was like a thick fog had descended into the halls, one so blinding that nobody could see anything but it.

Sara and Cathy were both still crying to Dr. Phillips, the guidance counsellor, while a shocked Mike gave statements to the police about what time Jamie had left last night.

Xander just watched, feeling terrible and guilty, thinking (if only in the back of his mind) that his wish had somehow caused this tragedy. He stared through the guidance counsellor's window at Sara as she bent over and buried her face in her hands, tears streaming down, and her eyes red and puffy. Her usually perfect blonde hair was a tangled mess from the number of times that she had run her fingers through it. Her blouse was wetted with the salt water pouring out of her eyes.

Cathy was crying too, but was still more composed than Sara. She managed to keep Dr. Phillips' gaze, nodding to his questions and comments at the appropriate times, only now and again bringing up a hand to wipe her runny nose. She let the tears fall, making no attempt to catch them. They just fell to the floor, softly pitting against the carpet.

Xander's gaze fell from them. He pictured Jamie's face, the way he had looked last year when the Cougars had won the semi-finals, his face filled with a transcendent joy. Or the way he looked the first time he and Greer Donaldson had danced at last year's spring formal. Or the way he'd sounded the last time they'd spoken, outside in the parking lot, when he had offered to walk home with him and Sara.

Sighing, he walked over to the nearest chair and collapsed into it. Leaning back, eyes closed shut, he banged his head off of a metal filing cabinet behind him.

"Ow," he said flatly, barely acknowledging it.

He opened his eyes and stared up at the ceiling. There were papers leaning over the side of the cabinet with police stickers on them.

Sticking out of a pale yellow folder amongst the files were pictures of Jamie.

Raising an eyebrow, he quickly glanced over at the police officer who was now talking with Tommy Irons. Biting his lip while he fought the urge to do it, he grabbed the file and stuffed it into his jacket, rising up from his chair and out of the counsellor's office.

Trying to remain as unseen as possible, something that he had become adept at over the years, he snuck through the halls and into the library. Hurrying to the back row of seats behind a bookshelf, he opened up the file and peered inside.

What he saw was horrific. The pictures depicted the last few moments of Jamie's life clearly. The rumors Xander had heard about the body had been true, and worse. His clothes were in shreds, especially the Cougars leather jacket he had cherished so much. The cloth that normally would have been silky was now rough and hard with dried blood. You couldn't really tell from the pictures, but he was sure he saw claw marks on him. His organs were all missing. Heart. Kidneys. Liver... everything except the lungs.

"What's that?" Mike said from somewhere in front of him.

Xander closed the folder quickly, but without arousing caution.

"Um... Lit Assignment."

"Ugh. Keep that crap away from me. I don't need anything like that right now," Mike droned as he sank down into a chair next to his friend. His face was flush white, his eyes distant and sad.

Good, thought Xander. "So how are you and Cathy getting along?" he chimed, understanding his friend's need to not talk about what was going on right now.

"Oh. Great. But this thing with... well, it doesn't help matters."

"Why? What's wrong?"

"It's Grendel. I know how she feels about him..."

"Yeah," Xander said calmly, getting up from his seat. "And she feels better about you. You know how lucky you are to have a girl like that love you?"

"Yeah, but..."

"But nothing. It's not worth the crap it'll cause for you two."

Mike frowned, then smirked a little. "I hate it when you're right, you know that?"

"Then you're just going to have to stop being so damn stupid all the time," Xander replied, slapping him on the back heartily.

"You wanna get a bite at Tiffany's?"

"Sure." They headed off, and Xander took one last look back at the pictures in the folder. "I don't think I'm gonna eat though. I haven't really got that much of an appetite today."

As much as we'd like to forget it sometimes, everyone remembers a death. Not only friends and loved ones, but also acquaintances. Even people we have never met will mourn our passing thanks to media, the internet, and word of mouth. Whether we like it or not, death is always a recorded event in our society.

Especially by the body experiencing it.

Be it for explanations natural or external, an examination of any cadaver will tell you how it came to be in that state. Every body has a story to tell, it just cannot form the words all on its own.

If the victim or victims were shot, there will be an entry wound of a certain size and depth depending on the weapon fired. It will tell us the positioning of the weapon, the victim, and the shooter. In some cases there is an exit wound and gunpowder residue as well, all of which can be used to reconstruct the events leading to the person's demise.

If the victim was strangled, veins in the eyes will appear bloodshot and pronounced.

If the victim was stabbed, taking a mold of the puncture wound can reveal the size, shape, and sometimes even the origin of the weapon used.

Hairs, slivers of glass, fibers, bug cocoons, defensive wounds and other foreign substances all contribute to figuring out how and under what circumstances death finally occurred.

"Coral Beach Precinct Morgue, Tuesday the twentieth. My name is Harry Ford. I'll be your mortician for this evening."

"Come on, Harry. Quit fooling around and start the tape. This guy's creepy," Lance Berkshire said to his partner. He scratched the few strands of remaining hair around his right ear, his stocky frame jittering a little as he did so. He always found it cold here, and just a little moist.

He stared down at what remained of Jamie Dawkins, struggling to sum up enough saliva to allow him to speak again. After a moment, he clicked on the tape recorder. The plastic gears spun the film around them for almost a full minute before he had gathered up enough courage to start. "Subject name: Dawkins R. Jamie. Male. Caucasian, five-five, two-hundred fifty-five pounds. Cause of death: undetermined. Hey Harry, pass me the scalpel."

Harry's hand convulsed as he picked up the thin ti-
tanium knife and handed it to his partner. The flippancy
known as Gallow's Humor he had clung to wavered for a
moment, as he found himself unable to tear his eyes away
from the vacant stare of their patient.

Lance began poking at the cold body, making one
clean slice to fully expose the thorax. He wouldn't have
to do much cutting though since the entire chest cavity
had been pretty much removed. There were rips and tears
around the edges of the hole the killer had made, each of
them with four distinct claw marks, that had made the
first officer on the scene think it had been an attack by a
wolf or a bear.

His final cuts made at the neck and pelvis, Lance braced
a hand on either side of the chest cavity and pushed. It
opened like a hinge in dire need of oiling, and the sound
it made was a wet suck followed by a snap. He looked at
the rib cage he had just forced open, which was now just
broken shards of bone, except for one which was smooth.

"Harry, look at this."

"What? It's a rib. So?" Harry said, raising an eyebrow
and leaning his lanky frame inward, peering down at
what Lance was indicating, a bit of his blonde hair falling
down into his eyes.

"So? Look at it. It's been perfectly sawed off, like it
was done with a tool. And look here," Lance said, making
a broad sweeping motion across the corpse's torso. "All
the body cavity organs have been taken, except the lungs.
They haven't even been touched. They even worked
around them to get to other organs. I don't know any ani-
mals that picky."

Harry maneuvered the light hanging from the ceiling to get a better look. "You mean a human did this? Something with a soul? Geez."

"That's what I think," he heaved, his frown seeming as though it were trying to escape the sides of his mouth. He checked a box and scribbled something down on his chart, his eyes darting back and forth to Jamie's open chest.

"What?" Harry asked, trying to follow Lance's gaze. "What is it?"

"The lungs are a bit dark."

"Probably a smoker."

"He's just a kid."

"Most smokers are."

Lance shot him a wry look, then laid down his clipboard and picked up his scalpel again. "Why weren't the lungs taken, anyway?" he asked rhetorically, fortifying one hand against the body's shoulder as he stuck his scalpel into one of the lungs. It resisted at first, the rubbery flesh bending inward against the pressure, then eventually opened with a slight hiss of air. He slid the knife down several inches, then put his blade aside and stuck in a gloved hand, stretching the organ until that part was inside out. Seeing the inside of the boy's lung revealed the blackness inside. It looked as though tar had been marinated into the meat. "Guess you were right. Looks like our Mr. Dawkins was actually a pretty heavy smoker. Our killer didn't want any damaged organs. Only the best."

Harry looked up, shivering a little as he felt the cold, sterile environment of the morgue get just a little bit colder.

ᚠᚤᚣ

The bathroom at the Factory was one of the filthiest in town, coming in second only to the bar on Spring Street.

The floors were a dark green tile and grew mold so fast that you could almost watch it, first starting in the gray hued cement that held one to the other around their edges, then slowly working its way in until the original colour was just an odd dot in the centre.

There was a space heater against the far wall that never worked, and would occasionally shoot radiant blue sparks at people walking by if there was enough water on the floor. It was a sickly nicotine yellow and always smelled like burning hair. If you looked inside the grate near its top, you could see bits of paper and beer stoppers that had been shoved inside by idle hands. Some were charred beyond recognition, others with simply singed along their edges. Once someone had found a hockey card lodged in there, wrapped in a plastic sleeve and in mint condition.

While there were no separate bathrooms for different genders, this had clearly been the boy's bathroom. There was a urinal not far from the heater that always stank of warm piss. It was stained a dark orange around the sides and near the bottom where it met the pipe. There were still little blue cakes placed in it every day (likely tossed in from a safe distance of several feet), but it had gone largely unused for almost two years. Very few men had wanted to put their manhood anywhere near its corroded porcelain surface.

The girl's room had been commandeered by the staff several years back, when they'd decided they no longer wanted to share a bathroom with their customers.

Sara let out a long, mournful wail as she stared at herself it the filthy mirror, trying to force herself to stop for the third time. More tears welled up and blocked her vision until she couldn't even recognize herself, her soft features coming out like a picture taken while someone had spread Vaseline on the lens.

She let out another long, baleful moan that turned into an "oh" sound, glancing back at the bathroom door nervously to make sure it was locked.

There were white, milky stains around the edges of the mirror. Her gaze found them again and again, no matter how hard she tried to look away.

She dabbed at her eyes with the stocking wrapped around her hand, clearing her vision again. She sniffed back, trying to stop her face as it insisted on leaking from every available crevice. She wiped her nose, so hard that her rings scraped against its tip and made it red.

"Fuck," she cursed, reaching down and retrieving her purse from her side and laying it on the edge of the sink. With trembling hands she worked the clasp, her vision becoming muddy and blurred again.

"Stop it!" she snapped at herself, finding her foundation and slamming it down on the sink.

She turned on the tap cautiously, only touching it with the tips of her fingers. It was just as dirty as everything else here was. There was a brown sticky substance on one end that had been there for months. The janitors avoided it as much as the patrons did.

The water that spouted from the tap was yellow at first, then slowly faded to a more normal shade. It never completely lost that hue, and gained something that again looked like diluted milk, but was serviceable.

She cupped her hands beneath and waited until they were full, then splashed it onto her face. It left a sour smell on her skin, but the cold was refreshing and brought her back to reality, at least for a moment.

When she looked at herself again the sparkling treads her tears had left were gone, but her nose was still red. The skin under her eyes was red too, and had become puffy and pronounced.

She huffed, unscrewing the top of her makeup and beginning to apply it methodically. In some odd way it soothed her, the way any familiar task soothed the weary. She'd been applying foundation in these same motions since she was eleven, and returning to it somehow brought her to a calm place. Not necessarily a place of peace, but a place where she could get lost in the routine of the mundane until the storm finally passed.

By the time she finished, she wasn't even sniffling anymore.

She looked back down into her purse.

There was an orange prescription bottle there that until a few hours ago had resided in her mother's medicine cabinet. It was filled with small blue pills with a diagonal indentation on the back. She watched it for a moment, as if expecting it to do something, then picked it up and popped the top off with her thumb.

She poured a handful of the little blue circles her mother called happy pills and her father called Valium into her hand, forming a neat little mountain in her palm. She looked at it again, wriggling her fingers and feeling the way they moved and shifted with her every motion, then poured them back into the bottle until there were only two left. Those two stared back at her like two pale eyes.

She turned on the tap again and was about to cup her other hand underneath to get enough water so she wouldn't have to dry swallow them, then stopped. She sighed and placed one back in the bottle. She held the other between her thumb and forefinger, hovering it over the bottle as if threatening to throw it back with the others.

Turning back to the door again, she sniffed back hard.

"Fuck it," she said, then pushed the pill between her pursed lips. She bent down and stuck her mouth into the stream of milky liquid coming out of the faucet, sucking back more than enough to make the pill go down easily. Her hair got wet as she did this.

She turned off the tap and placed the cap back on the bottle, then gave herself one last look in the mirror. She adjusted her bra strap so it wasn't quite so visible, then nodded approvingly and stepped toward the door.

When her hand touched the knob, her vision became hazy again. She paused, bit her lip, and forced herself not to start crying again.

To her surprise, it worked this time. She glanced at her reflection in the cruddy mirror one last time, forced a smile onto her face, then walked out of the bathroom and back out into the Factory.

She and Xander had decided to join Mike and Cathy that evening. They had agreed beforehand to walk home together, and nobody had blamed them. On their way there they had seen people affixing new locks to their windows, shops closing down early... and people only seemed to get more and more paranoid as they got closer to the club. Many older people gave them hard stares, following them with their eyes as they walked by.

Xander and Mike were caught deep in battle on an arcade game, which Mike appeared to be winning judging by the curses spewing from Xander's lips and the way he was rattling his joystick.

Cathy sat in the driving simulator, not actually playing it. She pried her eyes from Mike long enough to acknowledge Sara's return, but did not question her absence.

"What do you think of Grendel?" Sara asked, looking over at the buff hockey player.

"Ugh. I'm afraid to say. Mike's all upset over me and Gren. He won't accept that we're just friends," she tisked, pulling her hair back into a ponytail and tying an elastic in it.

"I meant for me."

Cathy rolled her eyes. "Don't you think it's a little soon? Kinda pushing it."

"Oh, yeah. The mourning has begun," she laughed. The smile she had practiced in the mirror was more natural now, and she herself did not know whether she was faking it or not.

Cathy laughed too, but only to be polite. She didn't see anything funny about it at all.

"Kick 'em! No! How'd you... argh!" Xander finally admitted defeat and stepped back from the joystick. "Dammit! How'd you do that last bit?"

"Well, it's all about a delicate balance of concentration, discipline, and not being a spaz. You wouldn't understand," Mike grinned as he straightened his collar.

"You're not a very good winner. Has anyone ever told you that?"

"Hmm," Mike responded, pretending to look thoughtful. "I don't know. You'd think I would be a better winner, what with all the practice I have."

Xander sighed, fumbling around his pockets for a quarter. Finding one, he held it up toward Mike at eye level, an evil grin spreading across his face. "Play again?"

"No way man. I gotta save some money to buy Cathy dinner."

Xander made a little sound like a whip under his breath.

"What was that?"

"I didn't say anything."

Mike eyed his friend for a moment. "One more game."

ʎϒ

Detective Carl Dent had seen his fair share of weird stuff. Sick stuff. The stuff that they leave out of even the worst horror flick, he lived every day of his life. Things that wake you up at night in cold sweats. Children massacred in hoards and piled up in men's sheds. People half eaten by some postal worker turned cannibal. Even a guy skewered on a lamppost. But when his commissioner passed him that folder, his gut turned over inside him. All he could think of was the sick, revolting, abhorrent nature of man.

He brushed a hand through his fast fading hair, briefly disrupting his comb-over before subconsciously putting it back into place. Flipping through the files on Jamie Dawkins, he felt himself unable to take his eyes away from the photographs or miss a single syllable written on the pages. He placed a hand over his mouth as he got to the part with close up photos of his organs, or where they should have been.

They had been extracted meticulously, with the preciseness and care of a practiced surgeon. The organs would be usable afterward if stored properly, if that was, in fact, the killer's intent. But the area *around* where the organs had been lifted was the exact opposite, slashed and mutilated and mauled. Like once the operation had been completed the person had purposely caused as much damage as possible to whatever remained, for no other reason than the pure, undiminished joy of it.

Worst of all, autopsy tests revealed that the victim may have been alive when the operation was happening. Or at least when it had begun.

Detective Tim White walked by Dent's desk, taking a peek over his shoulder at his friend as he did so. He frowned, his exaggerated lips and dark African-American complexion only bringing out the emotion more. "Jeez, Carl. What're you doing?"

Dent did nothing for a moment, so engrossed was he in the information in front of him. He seemed to be fixated on one photo, taken of the boy's lungs in the state they were in at the crime scene. Suddenly, his head snapped up to look at Tim, as if his reaction to his coworker's comment had been a delayed one. "Sorry. What?"

"Hard case?"

Dent emitted a low growl in the back of his throat.

"They're all hard. Especially when there's kids involved."

Tim nodded, prying his own eyes from the open folder. "I hear that. How old was he, anyway?"

"Eighteen."

"Ugh."

"What kind of monster could do something like this? And for what reason? There's just no logical sense behind it. This guy had no enemies, no grudges, he wasn't in a gang, there was nothing. He was clean."

"Maybe one of those idiot kids from the Cove?" Tim suggested, hating himself for saying it. "I mean, he was a star player. Maybe it's some kinda team rivalry."

"Yeah," Dent snorted. "And maybe they ate his organs to absorb his talent."

There was a look between them then as they both mentally examined the insanity and yet plausible validity of the comment, then brushed it aside.

"I'm glad you've got this one and not me," Tim admitted, tapping the top of Dent's cubicle wall once. "I don't think I'd be able to handle it."

Dent sighed, glancing back at the file. "Look at this: 'It is in the CS unit's professional opinion that the victim was attacked with a large, two-edged blade with a hilt, driven directly through the victim's right side.' I mean, that's a sword. That's a sword, right?"

"Or a machete."

"Who even does that? Really?"

"Dunno," Tim admitted reluctantly. "But I guess now it's your job to find out."

He gave his friend a curt wave then threw his jacket

over his shoulder and started toward the exit.

Carl watched him go, then picked up the file again, immediately re-absorbed in the disturbing photographs.

Sara stepped out in front of them, her shoes tapping along the sidewalk and her arms held just above her head as she turned the streetlight into a spotlight. Her jacket bobbed to the beat her feet created, flapping under her arms like the garments of some Broadway jazz dancer.

"What is she doing?" Mike laughed, walking slowly alongside Cathy and Xander. He'd been slapped on the arm by the former a few times already for walking too fast, his long legs making his strides command many more inches than theirs.

Cathy watched her for a moment, tilting her head to one side. "Hop scotch?"

"There's no squares."

"*Invisible* hop scotch then?"

"No, there's a beat to it. Watch."

Sara tapped and scuffed her feet as though she couldn't hear their critique, mouthing along to the song in her head as she did.

Xander smiled.

"It has a long body to it," Cathy said.

Mike nodded.

Sara continued to skip, the way her shoes worked along the pavement making different sounds, like morse code. Short short short short short short short, long long!

"Do do do do do do do, dah dah," Mike repeated, in time with her as she started again. "What is that?"

"It's Spirit in the Sky," Xander said finally, unable to keep his mouth shut any longer.

Sara stopped, spun around, and glared at him. "Tattler."

"They wouldn't have got it."

"Hey!" Mike spat, turning and pushing Xander with one finger. "It was on the tip of my tongue."

"Sure."

"It was!"

"Uh-huh."

Cathy laughed, entwining her fingers into Mike's as the three of them caught up to Sara and they began to walk in unison.

Xander paid particular attention to their legs for a moment. It seemed as though Mike, Cathy and Sara were unintentionally stepping in unison, like soldiers on the march. He tried for a moment to force himself to be in synch with them but could not and eventually gave up. Still, it nagged at him.

They walked like this often, most of the time with no particular destination in mind. On nice summer nights they'd walk from one end of town to the other, just enjoying one another's company and making fun of anything they saw that had amused them that day and complaining about how none of them had a car.

They turned down Xander and Sara's street, a long stretch of road that connected Norman's Lane to Laird Street. Their houses loomed in the distance, the lights in Xander's house all dark. From where they were, it looked abandoned.

All the lights were on in Sara's house, blaring out into

the night like it was on fire. Her mother's silhouette could be seen in the window, staring out into the street like a fisherman's wife looking out to sea.

Sara rolled her eyes. "I told her not to wait up."

"It's not even ten," Mike drawled. "I'd lay wages she was up anyway."

"You know what I mean."

"She's just worried," Cathy said, her voice smooth as silk. "Everyone is. Everyone should be."

"She's always like this. Ever since the crash," Sara continued, as though Cathy hadn't spoken. "This just gives her a good reason. Now I can't talk her out of it again."

"Pity," Xander smirked at her. "You might actually have to start being respectable."

She punched him in the arm even as she started laughing, and continued to laugh as she did it more and more. He raised his hands to try and defend himself, but kept lowering them to clutch his sides as rolls of laughter came out of him as well.

Cathy smiled, watching the two of them play. After a moment she leaned in and kissed Mike on the neck, the highest point she could reach without stopping in mid-stride and standing on her tip toes.

He smiled as her hair tickled his collarbone, squeezing her hand lovingly.

When they reached the walkway to Sara's house her mother opened the door, bathing the cobblestone in harsh bright light.

"Sara!" she snapped, her foot stomping a little when she did. It was a Johnson family trait, Xander had noticed, to talk with your feet. "You had me worried sick!"

"It's not even ten," Sara huffed as she walked toward her house, turning back to Mike as if to quote him. "Don't be such a drama queen."

"Don't take that tone with me, not after the other night. I have every right to be worried, and you know it."

She turned back to the rest of the group and smiled glumly, shrugged her shoulders, then entered her house without another word.

"This isn't a good time to be out and about like this," her mother continued, even as she closed the door. "I don't know how you can be so aloof when --"

The door closed, blotting out the light and muffling the sound of her scolding until they couldn't hear it at all.

Cathy sighed, then started walking again, towing Mike along with one hand.

Xander continued to watch the spot where Sara had disappeared for a moment, then stepped quickly to join them.

"Why do people say it like that?" he asked to no one in particular as they walked across the threshold into his yard. "I mean, we all know what happened. It'll probably even make the national news tonight. So why is everybody acting like it's some kind of a secret?"

"Because," Cathy explained, her silky voice singing through the cold night. "People don't like to know things like that. So they pretend they don't. Nobody likes to walk down the street, wondering what's behind them. But we do. Because if we don't... well..."

"Well, look what happened to Jamie," Mike finished, his eyes cast downward.

Xander paused, his head looming downward as he

pondered that for a moment, then reluctantly accepted it as fact. He gave a curt wave goodbye to Cathy and Mike when they reached his door, then walked into his house and up the stairs toward his room, not saying a word to wake his parents.

When he got to the top, he got a sharp pain in his right side and nearly fell, but caught himself on the rail. The pain went away as quickly as it had come over him, but even after it was gone there was a steady ache as he entered his room. It reminded him of when people lost their limbs in wars yet said they could still feel them, even though they were gone. Pausing for a second while he leaned on his desk to make sure that it had passed, he shrugged it off, thinking nothing of it beyond the moment. He wasn't terribly athletic and he had been walking for a while. Usually he'd get online after getting home, but tonight he felt tired. He could barely keep his eyes open, and Cathy had caught him yawning more than once on the walk home. He got to his room and was about to lie down when he thought he heard something off in the corner of his room, and suddenly he got very scared.

It's just the house settling, he told himself, but still he turned on the light and looked around. He checked under his bed and around the room. He found nothing, but then he heard the sound again behind him. He turned sharply.

The light bulb on his ceiling went out with a sudden flash and he was left in the dark, his eyes seeing spots everywhere.

His heart skipped a beat. He tried to swallow but it got stuck in his throat as sweat began to bead on his brow.

The sound, now that he actually listened, was like a long shuffle. Like someone trying to find something while scuttling about in the dark. There was the slight flicker of paper.

He stopped breathing to listen hard. He couldn't hear anything now, not even the usual sounds that the house made. He turned on the computer screen to give himself a little light, bathing the room in an eerie green glow. He stopped again to listen hard and heard it a second time, in the corner. He went over, pulled away a box and re-vealed... an old computer magazine flapping against his air conditioner.

He laughed at himself, breathing a sigh of relief. He walked over to his door and locked it, then got in his bed and slipped into a long, deep sleep.

ᑫᐧᐤ

As Xander Drew slept, Cathy and Mike walked down the street toward her house. They hadn't said much since leaving Xander's place. They both knew what was on each other's mind.

Jamie.

He had been Mike's friend, not Cathy's. So it was okay for Cathy to talk about it, but not okay for Mike to hear about it. What resulted was a weird sort of silence that made them both uncomfortable, and yet left them no way to escape from it.

There was a thick mist of fog rolling onto the streets.

Cathy stopped him on the corner by touching his arm and forcing him to face her, then leaned in slowly and kissed him. He kissed her back, only for a moment, and then they resumed walking across the road.

"So can we talk about it now?" she asked, the words coming with a sigh of relief that they had finally found their way free.

He took her hand in his own. "Not yet. It's still... too early."

"When then?"

He sighed, thinking ahead a little more than he usually liked to. "Um, how about at Grendel's party Saturday?"

"Three days?" she whined, pouting her lower lip. She didn't like holding things in. She was the type of person who said whatever was on her mind whenever she wanted. Not that she was a flake. Actually, she was the exact opposite. Those who knew her knew that she took responsibility for everything. She probably even blamed herself for Jamie's death in some way.

She leaned in to kiss him again, but they were interrupted by a sound behind them. Cathy jumped into Mike's arms and he laughed at her.

"What?" he asked, holding her lightly by the shoulders.

"I- I thought I heard a sound," she stammered.

He laughed at her again. "You could not be more cliché if you tried. You really think there's some crazed killer on the..."

Shink.

This time he heard it too. The sound of metal scraping on metal. They both stood perfectly still, neither making a sound.

Shink.

Again. Closer this time. It was coming from across the

street, around the corner that they had just come from.

"Come on," he said, taking her by the arm and they broke into a fast walk down the street toward her house. They rounded the next corner and stopped for a moment to listen. They could hear it.

Shink. Shink. Shink.

Metal scraping across the pavement, getting closer and closer to them. They broke into an all out run as they passed under a street lamp next to a gas station. Cathy stopped for a minute and banged on the windows as she went. "Help us!" she screamed to arouse the curiosity of anyone who might be inside, but there was no response.

Mike stopped a few feet past her, turning around when he heard the noise she was making, the expression on his face turning from unadulterated fear to pity for just a moment.

She stared into the tinted windows of the station, only the night lights on to let her see that everyone had left, every business had closed early. Everyone in this town had been spooked by Jamie Dawkins' death. So the two were alone. Her lower lip shook as her eyes searched frantically amongst the dimly lit potato chip and cigarette displays for any sign of movement, desperation beginning to pump through her fragile body as fast as adrenaline.

Shink.

Mike jogged back toward her, taking her firmly but gently around her upper arm. "Come on. We don't have time," he said, his voice the only part of him showing his exhaustion.

She looked around the gas bar again, her hair whipping around her head, when the sound came again.

Shink.

It was so close she thought she had felt the blade graze the goosebumps on the back of her neck. She started to run with Mike again without even looking where he was leading her, taking off away from the abandoned station and back onto the street toward her home.

Mike turned around momentarily, looking into the gaping darkness through the thick fog. He heard the sound again, followed by a sight. The gleam of a long, curved piece of metal shining in his eyes. He turned back toward the front, the voice of his junior high gym coach ringing in his ears, telling him to keep his eyes facing forward. You run faster when you're facing forward.

Cathy didn't get far before she buckled over in pain. They'd been walking for hours, and now all this running had produced a spasmodic ache in the muscles of her stomach, sending shots of agony down her legs and upwards into her chest. She tried to get up, but her body automatically cried out in rebellion sending her back down to her knees. Mike looked back again.

Nothing.

He helped her to her feet and listened for a moment. Then, from the darkness, something slashed at her.

"Ah!" she cried, as she felt the heat of pain rip up and down her thigh. Something had tried to cut through her hamstring. She quickly propped herself onto Mike's shoulder and then began to run, but Mike knew it was hopeless. She was hopping around on one foot, and he wouldn't be able to take her added weight for too much longer.

When he looked over his shoulder again, he saw it. A tall, dark figure steadily making its way toward them. It wasn't running, and yet it was making progress on them. With a single thought of horrible brilliance, a light went on in Mike's head and he realized that they both wouldn't make it. He stopped when they passed the next corner, a shocked look on his pasty white face.

The guy was close; they both knew it. Cathy's house was only about a block away, but they wouldn't make it. They both knew it.

"Why are you stopping?" she asked, wide eyed with astonishment and pain, tears already streaming down her face.

Holding her arms with both hands, he pulled her in and kissed her, then pushed her in the direction of her house. "Go."

She started to cry fresh tears, but turned and ran toward her home.

Mike turned around to face their attacker. Suddenly, he felt a sharp pain in his right side as a long, double-edged sword plunged into him. He screamed as the attacker twisted the blade slightly before ripping it out again. Mike felt his blood flow freely from the wound. He turned. He wanted to know. *Had* to know who this mysterious figure was before he died.

But there was no one there. He was alone.

He turned and ran for Cathy's home. The pumping of his legs increased the blood flow, and as her house came into sight, he started to feel light headed. He stopped for a moment on a bench to catch his breath. He put his hand on his side and pressed, shooting pain all through his torso. He looked down at his hand, soaked in blood, looking black in the darkness of the night street. Closing his eyes, he let his head rest a minute. Then he remembered what they tried to tell you on those medical shows that he and Xander loved so much. When you got a wound like this, you don't close your eyes. There's a good chance that you'll never wake up again.

So he clenched his teeth and got up.

He fell immediately to the sidewalk, skidding his knees against the concrete. He vomited onto the gray stone, but then realized that it was blood, its coppery taste filling his mouth and throat. Mike had always hated the taste of his own blood, and now he was drowning in it. He wrapped his hands around his sides, trying desperately to stop the stream of red fluid coming from them.

CHAPTER THREE
INJECTED

"Mike? Dear God, Mike?" came a voice from ahead. The sound was muffled by the throbbing pain in his skull. It sounded like someone talking while underwater.

Mike looked up. Even his vision had begun to get hazy, but he could plainly see Cathy's dad coming toward him. He was a hard man to mistake for anyone else. David Kennessy was portly and kind of shaped like a pear, with saggy jowls that shook whenever he spoke. His eyes always looked kind and often concerned, as they did right now as he looked down at the open wound on Mike's side.

Mike only grunted in response.

"Oh, fuck," he said as he picked Mike up and put his arm around his shoulder. "Let's get you into the warm, son."

The walk back to the house was both slow and rushed at the same time. With every agonizing step they took, David could feel the boy in his arms tremble. He could see the blood as it continued to soak through his shirt at an alarming rate, faster than he would have thought possible.

He'd never seen that much blood before, not in real life.

There was a sound behind them and David pressed forward, glaring back between them with eyes filled with fear. Mike kept up the new pace for only a moment, then let out a long grunt and slowed down. David obliged. It was like trying to run a three-legged race when the prize is your life and your partner was a toddler.

"M'sorry," Mike hummed painfully.

"It's okay," David said, patting him on the chest.

It wasn't.

They made their way to the house without incident, David opening the door with a firm kick. The latch had never been good, and opened with even the slightest force.

Cathy and her mother, Karen, were still on the couch crying. There were first-aid bandages in place on Cathy's calf, and Karen had just hung up the phone with the hospital. When she heard the door open, she got up and yelled: "David? Dear god, did you find him?"

Then she saw him. She gasped at the sight of the boy she loved like her own son with his clothes and hands drenched in blood. She hurried Cathy upstairs despite her screams and cries of protest.

They laid Mike onto the couch, placing pillows under his neck and head to prop them up. David wrapped some makeshift bandages tightly around his torso to stop the bleeding, and placed blankets on him to keep him warm. They could hear the ambulance's siren in the distance.

Cathy gave up fighting her mother and went into her room, slamming the door behind her so hard it rattled pictures all over the house. There was only a second's worth of silent pause before they heard her scream.

All eyes in the room went wider than ever, a difficult feat considering the situation.

David looked from his wife to Mike and then back again before he rushed up the stairs, leaving Mike momentarily to see what was wrong. Karen followed.

He reached his daughter's room and opened the door. He found his daughter curled into a ball on the floor next to her double bed, crying and holding her legs tightly against her body. She peered over her knees with panic stricken eyes, unable to pry her gaze off the foreign object in her room.

There was a long, double-edged sword sticking out of her floor. It had golden lining and a rubber handle in the middle, and was perfectly clean. No blood was on it.

David ran to the window and looked out. There was nothing there except the ambulance pulling up, its flashing red lights making eerie shadows on the street. He turned to his wife and daughter. "Did he hurt you?"

"There was nobody h-here. Just the... the thing," Cathy stammered hysterically.

David turned and looked at the blade, put in so little time ago that it was still wobbling like a tuning fork.

"How could someone have sunk that in without anyone hearing?" he breathed to himself.

He ran back downstairs, leaving his wife and child in the room. He thanked God that his younger daughter was staying at a friend's house.

He greeted the paramedics quickly and led them into the living room, where Mike was drifting in and out of consciousness. One of the younger medics lifted up the blanket and looked at the wound as they hefted him onto the stretcher.

"Fuck," he mumbled so that only he could hear. "Gutted like a friggin' fish."

They rushed him into the ambulance and began work right away, giving him morphine for the pain as they tried urgently to staunch the blood flow. Cathy got into the van with him. She had wounds to treat as well. She started to bawl as she saw the blank look in her boyfriend's eyes, which were faded and rolled back into his skull. The doctors began to stitch up the wound before they even arrived at the hospital. They rushed him into emergency as Cathy went into a smaller doctor's office. It was the first time she wondered if she would ever see him again. And for a while, the only sound she could hear was her own heart breaking.

Xander woke up the next morning and stretched, scratching his sides. He heard the familiar crack of his bones and the creak of his bed as he got up, his skin still sticky and clammy from the warm night's sleep. He went over to his computer, whose alarm clock program was beeping the "time to wake up" song it played every day at seven. He jiggled the mouse to get rid of the saver, then clicked the off button on the beeping clock.

He hauled on a new shirt and jeans and opened his door. He stopped dead in his tracks, staring at the door, his lower lip quivering just a little.

His door had been locked last night. Now it wasn't.

He looked around his room quickly for anything out of the ordinary and saw nothing. Just stacks of Popular Science magazines and clothes scattered all over the floor, along with a pile of CDs he'd been meaning to give back to Sara for some time. Taking a long, slow pan of the room to make sure, he decided that it had to be nothing. Maybe the lock had slipped, as it had sometimes in the past. No big deal.

He walked down the stairs and into the kitchen. He turned sharply to see his mother crying and his father sitting at the table.

Xander's father was old and scrawny, wearing a flannel shirt and suspenders he refused to admit were out of style. His shoulders were slumped forward and his face sagged more than usual as he clenched his wife's hand tightly around her fingers.

She was a little younger and usually hid her years much better. Today her hair wasn't curled and Xander noticed she was only wearing one earring. The makeup on her round face was smeared by tears and tissues, and when she looked at Xander he could see her eyes were bloodshot.

Xander's eyes widened in shock. "What's going on?" He almost didn't need to ask. It was as if he knew before the words even escaped his mother's lips. The image of what he knew had happened came to his brain. He could practically hear her saying the words in her head.

"Xander, son, you should sit down," his mother coaxed, motioning toward an empty chair at the table.

"No. No way. Just fucking tell me," he said slowly but defiantly, hating it when people started bad news with sit down. It just made it worse by drawing it out.

"Sit," his father said in a stern voice, frowning in disapproval of his son's choice in language.

Xander took a step toward the chair without even realizing it, almost as a reflex, his father glaring at him as he did.

"Alex, sweetie, were you with Mike and Cathy last night?" his mother asked, her voice unwavering even through her tears.

"I... what?" Xander asked, getting confused as his head spun a mile a minute.

"Son, Michael and Cathy were attacked last night," his father said bluntly, placing an open palm on the table as if he were laying out the facts.

Xander could feel the words cut through him like a dagger. He ran into the porch and hauled on his shoes, unlocked the front door and ran out.

His mother started to get up and go after him, but his father touched her on the arm quickly, shaking his head.

He hopped across the threshold they had passed over only last night. He ran to Sara's doorway and started banging on her door.

She opened it, still wearing her nightgown, her eyes red and puffy.

Without a word, he took her into his arms and cried.

Carl Dent slammed a fist down on the folder in front of him, this one marked Harris/Kennessy. "Fuck!" he yelled, getting the attention of the entire wing. Nobody dared to say anything to him, as the entirety of his balding head turned red with livid anger.

He ran a hand through his remaining hair, clenching his teeth as he opened both this and the Dawkins file.

"What am I missing?" he mumbled to himself, waiting for something to jump out at him. A tattoo, a locale, anything besides the manner in which the people were attacked.

Suddenly, his phone rang.

He glared at it, willing it to stop on its own.

Which of course, it did not.

Cursing again, he picked it up and put it to his ear. "Dent," he grumbled, scraping his teeth together.

"Yes, this is Don Smith. I'm a reporter with Beach News Daily..." said the polite yet exhausted voice on the other end of the line.

Dent rolled his eyes, throwing his free hand up in the air. He hated reporters, always had. More than anything, he hated the way they introduced themselves, putting emphasis of their job title, the newspaper, and even their name. It was as if they were trying to make themselves sound so much more important than they really were. "Yes?" he sighed reluctantly.

"... I was wondering if you had any information regarding the attack?"

"All information associated with Jamie Dawkins that we are willing to disclose at this time has been released in a press release to all media outlets. I would suggest you get off the phone with me and check your fax machine. Besides, I only deal with Tom Drake. He's the only decent reporter at that rag."

There was an audible silence on the line as Don took a deep sigh, composing himself before speaking again. "I wasn't talking about that attack. I meant the attack last night. On Mike Harris and Cathy Kennessy?"

Dent raised an eyebrow. "And how do you know shit about that?"

"My son told me. He goes to their school. They all seem to know..."

Dent narrowed his eyes. "Then why don't you go ask them?" he hissed, slamming the phone down onto its receiver as hard as he could.

He immediately grabbed the file on Mike and Cathy and threw on his jacket, cursing as he walked toward the door.

"Bout time I stopped sitting on the sidelines anyway..." he mumbled, slamming the door behind him.

ᚠ⋎ᚠ

Xander and Sara both took that Wednesday off school to go visit Mike and Cathy in the hospital. Cathy was as good as new. The blade had only breached the skin.

Mike was a different story. The killer's blade had punctured the right side of his abdomen and gone in several inches. The flesh there had required fifty-two stitches and ten staples to stay closed. The blade had missed the major organs, although the attending physician still was not sure how. It had ruptured one organ however, nearly slicing it half and resulting in its immediate removal from Mike's body.

"Your appendix?" Sara repeated, fighting to control

her laughter. "Some people have to pay to get that useless ball of flesh removed, and you're all whiny cause some creep did it for free?"

Mike laughed weakly at that, feeling his stitches stretch. He knew she was joking. "Ha. Yeah, guess it is kinda funny when you look at it like that. If you're a twisted freak like you are."

Cathy did one of her famous fake laughs, then gave Mike a kiss on the cheek.

"The doctors even say if I rest up, I'll be out of here in time for Grendel's party," Mike added happily, squeezing his girlfriend's hand tightly and giving her a happy smile.

"Great. Perfect," Xander joked cheerfully. "But I think Cathy's going to be disappointed. She was looking forward to some alone time with ol' Gren."

Both Sara and Cathy laughed at that. Mike did not.

Xander coughed awkwardly. "Well, if you feel up to it later, I think I spotted an arcade down near the waiting room. Maybe they've got --"

"Nope," Mike cut him off. "Sorry buddy, our game isn't there."

"Dammit," he whined, stomping his foot dramatically.

"They've got Marble Mutant Super Heroes though."

"Cool enough, I guess," he shrugged, scuffing his feet along the tile floor in disappointment.

There was a knock at the door and a tall, important looking man stepped into the room. He wore a cheap black suit and a leather tie. He had a dulled toothpick between teeth that looked jaundice, which he took out when he entered the room and flicked into the medical waste bin on the wall. His eyes were small and beady. They glared down Xander before even meeting with anyone else. He had a bad comb-over and cheeks that were just a little chubby, but not overly so. He reached into his suit and produced a badge, let it gleam brightly in the light from the window, then shoved it back.

"I'm Detective Carl Dent. Is this..." he looked at his papers, quickly finding the name he was looking for, "Mike Harris' room?"

"Yeah, that's me." Mike paused after speaking, breath catching as his side ached at him.

"He's the one in the bed," Sara smirked. "I think that should have been obvious."

"That's Sara, and this is my girlfriend Cathy. Can we... help you?" Mike continued, as though Sara hadn't spoken.

"Yes. I need to ask you a few questions regarding your attacker. Do you mind, or would you like me to come back later?" he smiled politely, again shooting a look at Xander.

Xander raised his eyebrows in response, not knowing what he had done to upset the man.

"No, now's fine," Mike smiled, then added quickly, "Oh! As long as you don't mind my friends being here."

Dent looked down on Xander again, this time making long eye contact.

"Not at all," he smiled. "Now I've worked on cases like this before, and I know you may have trouble spelling out the details over and over... so, all I want for the moment is a description on your attacker."

"I wouldn't be able to tell you. We never really saw him," Cathy replied solemnly.

"And you, sir?" He pointed with his pen to Mike.

"Same story."

"So, you're telling me you saw nothing, even though my report says you were stabbed under a street light?"

"Yes, sir," Mike said through barred teeth.

"And then the killer had to go past your girlfriend's oncoming father and get into her room, plant the sword in her floor (which would have been loud), all without making a sound and then get out again?"

"If that's what he said happened," Sara interrupted, "then that's what happened."

"I didn't ask you," he snapped curtly.

"Hey!" Xander jumped from his seat and glared into the detective's eyes. "What do *you* think happened?"

Dent took a deep breath and closed his folder. "I think that these last two attacks were gang related. The same stupid town pride crap that's been happening between here and Coral Cove for years. And that you made up these stories, maybe even stabbed each other, to protect a friend in the gang that you know did it."

Mike tried not to laugh. And failed.

Xander got up in Dent's face again and gave him a little shove. Not enough to get him in any kind a trouble, just a rude nudge, finding a backbone that he never even knew he had as the hairs on the back of his neck stood on end.

"Get out," he said simply, cocking his head toward the door.

"Okay," Dent said as he raised his hands up in defeat

calmly. "But I think I've got my gang banger right here." He motioned toward Xander and walked away.

There was a long silence even after he left the room.

"What a jerk," Cathy said after what felt like forever. She sat down on the bed next to Mike and kissed him.

Still the others were quiet.

"Come on!" she said in a more cheerful voice, getting out a wheelchair for Mike. "Let's go down to that game room like Xander said."

At Coral Beach High School, everyone was scared out of their minds. People were going crazy. There were wild rumors spreading all over the hallways now, with each student putting their own spin on what had happened and who had done it. Everyone had been blamed -- every student, every teacher, everyone that was known to be blamed had been blamed. There had even been recurrences of an old urban legend involving a man with hooks for hands that preyed on kids that went behind the Factory to make out at the kissing stone. In any case, students and parents alike were freaked. Every shadow was a killer, every movement a danger. Every sound was someone waiting to slice them open. And the teachers' suggestions to get a walk home buddy didn't help either.

Grendel roamed the hallways after his fourth period English class had gotten too boring. He had a slight smirk on his face, the satisfaction he always got after he'd done something he knew he shouldn't have. The halls were empty, and eerily quiet. Only the squeak of his footsteps on the wet floor could be heard. After a while the squeak wore off, and he had renewed hope that the principal would not catch him.

He heard the sound of scuffed, smooth shoes and recognized them immediately as Principal Shnieder's. He was a fat little troll of an administrator with ears that wriggled when he talked about geography and *only* when he talked about geography.

And he *loved* giving out detention slips.

Grendel ducked into the boy's bathroom just as Shnieder was coming around the corner, feeling his heart jump up into his chest when he did.

Tommy and 'Sud' were in the bathroom, where they spent most of their classes.

"What's up, Gren?" Tommy said in the halfway-mocking tone he almost always used. He was tall for his age at almost six foot five, and spiked his hair to add even a little more height. His grin seemed to stretch beyond the borders of his face as he greeted Grendel, opening his jean shirt to reveal a 'Hello Nasty' tee underneath. Sud sat next to him on the sink counter, scratching the stubble that composed his hair. He was a larger boy wearing a sweater even though he was clearly warm and his arms seemed a little too long for the rest of his body. He did not greet Grendel, but that was normal. Sud almost never spoke, except to back up Tommy.

"Nothin' much, man," Grendel replied, still listening for Shnieder to pass as he slapped hands with Tommy. "You guys still coming to my party this Saturday? It's gonna be a wild one."

"Yeah. Yeah, we'll be there," Tommy smiled, then dropped his voice, even though there was nobody else around. "Have you, ah, made your move with Cathy yet?"

Grendel lowered his voice too. "Not yet. I'm gonna do it at the party. I figure after all this Jamie business, and with Mike in the hospital, she'll need a shoulder to cry on."

"Yeah, and then a person to lie on."

They all laughed.

"Hopefully," he smirked, licking his tongue against his teeth. They stopped talking as they heard Shnieder pass the bathroom and continue around the corner. "Well, I gotta go. It's only so long before he checks in here. Talk to you later, guys."

Grendel stepped out into the quiet hallway once again. His shoes made no sound now.

Then suddenly, they did.

He stopped, but the squeaking continued for a moment or two. He put his back to the corner and poked his head out to check for Shnieder.

The halls were clear.

He looked back from where he came to see if it was Tommy or Sud coming out of the washroom, but that hall was clear as well. He began to walk again, and again the squeaking started, out of synch with his own footsteps. Then he heard it.

Schenk.

The sound of cold metal on the stone walls of the school. His body broke out in gooseflesh as he began to run up the halls toward his classroom. The sound and the squeaks sped up as well. He rounded the second-to-last corner to his class, and slipped on the floor, ploughing into the wet floor sign and then slamming into the lockers. Hard.

He picked himself up as he heard the squeaks, still coming now even though he had stopped. He heard the sound again, and suddenly remembered the rumors of the man with hooks for hands. He broke into a run, turning the next corner and running right into Carl Dent.

"What the hell are you doin', boy?" Dent bellowed.

"N-nothing," Grendel stammered as he looked down at Dent's metal coat strap, clinking against the wall, and sighed at his own silliness.

"I should report you to your --" Dent stopped for a moment, looked in his folder, then back up at Grendel. "Is your name Julian Grendel?"

"Uh, yeah. That's me. It's just Grendel though."

"Son, do you know an Alex Drew?"

"You mean Xander?"

"Come with me, boy."

"Son," Dent said as he glared at the boy from across the guidance counsellor's table. "How well do you know this... Xander, is it?"

"Yeah. He's all right. I invited him to a party coming up Saturday."

"So, you'd say that you were friends?"

"More like a friend of a friend," Grendel said, mulling the term 'friend' around in his head for a second.

"You mean Michael Harris?" he pushed, checking his file just to be sure of the name.

"Mmm. More like Cathy Kennessy," he corrected

quickly, a sly grin prying over his lips.

"I see. Alright, how would you describe Xander Drew?"

"He's cool enough. He knows what goes on. A little bit of a loner though."

"What do you mean?" Dent picked up his pen and paper and began to write.

"Well, he mainly only hangs around with these three people..."

Dent again looked at his notes. "Mike Harris, Cathy Kennessy and Sara Johnson."

"Yes." Grendel was starting to get a little freaked about how much Dent knew about the life of an average kid. "And when he's not shooting pool with them, he's usually inside on his computer. Guy fancies himself a bit of a hacker."

"So he keeps to himself a bit."

"Um, yeah. A little, I guess. Acts like he doesn't have the time of day for anyone else then wonders why they ain't got it for him. Truth is, if Sara didn't like him so much, he wouldn't be coming near my place this Saturday. Dunno what she sees in the guy."

Dent gathered up his papers, smiling from ear to ear. "Thank you for your help, son."

Grendel furrowed his brow, getting up the same time that Dent did, more than a little confused. "Wait, I thought you were going to ask me what I knew about the murderer?"

"I just did," he said under his breath, heading toward the door.

Grendel's mouth went slack, then turned up into a

grin.

"Well, this is just... neat," he cackled, turning toward the door himself.

"Son of a bitch!" Xander screamed as Mike's character laid another triple punch combo into his. "Even in a damn wheelchair he manages to beat me!"

Xander had chosen the Granite Gladiator, a gray behemoth wearing armor that made him look like Russell Crowe, thinking his brute strength would more than make up for his own inexperience with the game. He was wrong, as per usual. Against the strength and speed of Mike's character, the Stone Spider, the Gladiator was all but helpless. Mike did a half swivel with the joystick and pressed 'punch' three times in succession to initiate the 'Ultimate Spider' move, where the Spider just zipped around the screen, hitting the Gladiator about a hundred times as he went. The Granite Gladiator went down for the second time and the gold letters "Stone Spider Wins" appeared on the screen. The digital spider creature made the remark that the loser would 'Make a good sidekick.' With Xander's defeat the game went into one player mode and Mike fought the computer's character, randomly chosen as Obsidian. The scrawny little black statue came to life and leaped into the playing field, sprouting four sparkling claws at the end of each wrist as he did so.

"Dammit. I can't beat this guy," Mike muttered as Obsidian started off with something called a 'Hazard-O' attack, swirling his claws all around the screen in great gaping circles.

Xander wandered over to where the girls had been sitting, cursing all the way.

"Hi guy," Cathy said to him, "Get bored of the game?"

"Naw. Just bored of losing the game. But I think it cheered Mike up."

"Good." She leaned over and gave her friend a little kiss on the cheek. "Thank you."

"Whatever. If you need me, I'll be playing pinball," he said, motioning to where that game stood. "It's easier to take losing against a small metal ball. Mike's victory dance is even more demeaning when he's in that damn chair."

She giggled, knowing exactly what he was talking about.

"Kay," she said cheerfully, watching him as he made his way over to the pinball machine, digging change out of his pocket along the way.

With Xander gone, the girls could resume their talk. Cathy turned back to Sara, a concerned look upon her face.

"What do you think that investigator guy meant when he accused Xander of being in a gang?" Sara asked out of the blue, as she was known to do every now and again.

"I don't know. Maybe he thinks it's him because you and him were the only two people who knew that Mike and I were on that road."

A look of panic flashed across Sara's face, and her voice had a little more edge in it. "Hey, what makes you so special? Why would he think that you were actually targeted, instead of just a random victim like Jamie?"

"I don't know," Cathy said, just taking a sip of her soda. "But you damn well better hope someone figures it out. I don't know how Mike got away from that guy, but he was absolutely brutal."

"Argh!" Mike said, slamming his hands against the machine. Even Cathy noticed. The computer-controlled Obsidian had just finished him off with a move called 'Insanity Rage', and Stone Spider went spinning into the air before landing on his back with a thump. Mike wheeled himself over to where Xander stood searching his pockets for change after losing another quarter to the pinball game.

"That one's impossible, man," he said to his friend, motioning toward the air hockey tables. "Let's try our hand at a real sport."

Xander grabbed the handles on the wheelchair and put him in place at one end.

"Two paddles?" Xander asked, picking them both up and displaying them to his friend.

"Of course. But I'll use one. I figure with the wheelchair, and the one paddle, that'll mean I won't *totally* kick your ass."

"Hardy har," he said, throwing Mike his second paddle and putting a dollar into the side of the machine. It slowly buzzed to life.

"So, you are still going over to Grendel's... right?" Sara asked, almost out of boredom. "I mean, it is the social event of the season." She did a mock British accent when she said that, but it sounded more like Australian.

Cathy laughed at the horrifically bad impression, then brushed a strand of her long black hair back behind her ear. "I want to," she said, but there was that implied 'but' at the end of it, one that was left hanging there open-ended for Sara to pick up and follow on.

"So, why won't you? And don't give me any of that 'Mike thinks Gren wants me' crap either."

"I dunno," Cathy mulled, fiddling her straw up and down in her drink. "Don't you think it's possible? I mean, he does come off a little..."

"He doesn't," Sara assured her, placing one hand on her friend's knee to emphasize the sentiment. "Take it from someone who dated him. If he liked you, you'd know it."

"Really?" Cathy frowned, still visibly unsure.

"Absolutely," Sara laughed. "And even if he does, Gren's cool. He'd never act on it. Gren's good at keeping secrets. His own, and other peoples."

"I'm telling you guys. Xander Drew is the *killer*!" Grendel shouted. A small legion consisting of Sud, Tommy, Derek and a few others had gathered around him as he stood on one of the picnic tables outside school. "That guy from the cops practically *said* it!"

"No way," Tommy muttered under his breath, his eyes widening as he thought of all the times he and Xander had talked in the halls, or passed him in the stalls, or let him copy his history notes.... The thought made him shudder. "There's just *no way*." He smoothed a hand through his spiked hair, frazzling it as he played with the settings on the camera that hung relaxed around his neck.

"Yeah," echoed Sud, moving to fiddle with his own

hair as Tommy had, only to remember that his head was, in fact, shaved. He quickly brought his hand down, hoping that nobody had noticed. "No way."

"Anyway," Grendel continued, giving Sud a look that completely disregarded his last comment. "The evidence is all there! He hated Jamie because Sara liked him. Everyone sees the way he chases her around, been doing it since he was six goddamn years old. He tried to kill Cathy and Mike because he's angry at them for ditching him all the time. He sees what they've got and he knows he's never going to have that with Sara. Plus, he's the only one who knew where they would be that doesn't have an alibi. I mean, think about it. I couldn't accept it at first either but... no, just *think* about it and you'll see it."

"Yeah," Derek piped up. He shrugged, his black plastic jacket making ruffling sounds as he did. "And while we're at it, we'll all think about how the hell that whiny little weakling could even punch somebody enough to hurt them, let alone do any damage." He shrugged his shoulders again and walked away from Grendel.

"Yeah," Tommy said, ignoring Grendel's protests as he followed Derek's lead and walked back toward the bathrooms.

"Yeah," Sud said, mimicking Tommy's exact movements.

Grendel just got down off of the table as the rest of the crowd dispersed. He sat back, a look of hatred and darkness in his eyes.

You'll all pay for this, he thought. *Nobody ignores Julian Grendel.*

ᚠᚤᚠ

"Hey Dent," Tim said as he slipped on his suede jacket. "Find anything connecting those kids yet?" He smiled at Dent. The man was dedicated, that was for certain. He'd never let go of a case like this, not until he brought in the killer.

"No. Not yet," Dent admitted, not even looking up from the photos comparing Mike and Jamie's wounds.

"You should go home. Get some rest," he remarked, a faint sound of concern in his voice. "Fresh eyes would do that case better then tired ones."

"Tim, there have been two teen attacks in the last two nights. Tonight could mean another one for this killer. This kid may not be as lucky as the last two."

"Yeah, and it's an hour before sunset," Tim sighed, motioning toward the open window with his head.

Dent looked down at his watch in genuine astonishment. He had completely lost track of time. "Man oh man oh... wait."

Tim's eyes went up. "What?"

"I'd probably need another victim to prove this theory, but both Harris and Dawkins were adopted."

"Come on, Carl," Tim said, sighing as he shook his head at his friend. "So are thousands of kids all over America. You're grasping at shadows. What about the Kennessy girl?"

"She could have been just an innocent, in the way of the killer's attack."

"I think I liked your gang theory a little better. Besides..." his voice trailed off for a minute as he looked out the window at the sun. "It is now fifty-five minutes to sunset. I don't think you have time to run birth records on every kid in this town before then."

Dent cursed under his breath, running his hand over his mouth as he watched the sun slowly set. He glared at the bright orange orb as if it had betrayed him horribly.

"It's going to happen again, you know," he said finally, in a defeated, barely audible tone.

"Yeah," Tim reciprocated, pulling up a chair next to him. "I know."

"Dammit!" Xander yelled as Mike won his third straight game of air hockey. Xander had won the first game, but once Mike had gotten a handle on playing in the wheelchair, there was no hope. Goal after goal -- Mike had just hammered them in without remorse.

"I guess that means I win... doesn't it?" Mike gloated, getting as much enjoyment out of the moment as he possibly could.

"Get up out of that chair. You've gotta be milking it or something."

They all laughed. Cathy came over and gave Mike a short kiss, and there was an awkward pause between Xander and Sara.

"Ugh," Xander let out a little grunt.

"What is it?" Cathy asked, coming to his side.

"Um..." he paused for a second, putting pressure on his right side. "It's nothing. Really, it happened last night too. It's just a lot of pain in my right side."

Mike's eyes widened momentarily. *Could it actually be some kind of... sixth sense humans had to danger?* he thought, his mind going a mile a minute. *Was it possible that the killer was close by, in the building even.... no. God no, of course it wasn't.* He laughed at himself as he took Cathy in his arms again. Coral Beach was a big enough place that whoever this sicko was he didn't need to come looking for his targets.

"Come on," Sara chimed. "We have to call our parents if we're gonna be home in time for dinner."

⋏⋎⋏

Xander got home at around quarter to six. It was only just beginning to get dark. He ran up the stairs two steps at a time, knowing that his dinner would be waiting for him in his quiet room at the top. He opened the door and the smell of fried chicken made his mouth water. He sat down next to it and turned on the computer, taking a copy of the Beach News Daily that his mother had left on the keyboard and tossing it to one side.

Taking a sip of his coke from the large cup, he started browsing through his files looking for something to do.

He decided to check out that website that Soul had been talking about.

What was it called?

He took a big bite of gravy-covered chicken breast and licked his fingers, then checked his computer's chat history, pulling up the conversation he'd had with Soul earlier.

"**hello Pinkerton.**

Oh. Hi soul. How's life?

Alright. I've been looking at something weird online. I discovered some kind of bizarre... thing. I don't

have a password decoder as sophisticated as you do, I thought you might wanna take a look at it.

Sure. What's the site?

Something called engen.com. Oops. Gtg!

'got to go'?, why?"

"There," he said to himself, reading aloud off of the screen. "Engen.com."

He punched the address into his computer's web browser. Automatically, odd midi music started to play. A badly done gif animation of what he could only assume was the Engen logo came up onto the screen. It was a blue circle with a spike running through it from side to side, containing the word 'Engen'. When that was done, the main home page loaded up. It was filled with a bunch of different links going down the side, stuff like music, comic books, novels, the names of a few people he didn't recognize... all the trademarks of a well-designed and never visited personal web site.

"Welcome to Engen.com," a muffled voice recording said loudly, forcing Xander to turn down the volume on his control panel. "Your one-stop location for all MP3's and other music files, comic book updates, and everything else you could have read on the side bar, you illiterate fool." Then the voice went away and was replaced by a looping midi rendition of *Highway to Hell* by AC/DC.

Xander wasn't all too impressed. He was expecting some kind of freaky government place.

"But why would Soul need a decoder for this place?" He frowned, his eyes darting over the information presented. He scrolled down further. The site seemed to go on forever, with links to every torrent and hack he'd ever heard of.

Music by title, music by artist, music by style, music by date, music by era... the list seemed endless. Then he saw a little symbol on the bottom right-hand corner of the screen, set apart from the menu. Someone would have to scroll down a long time after the menu had ended to have even noticed it.

"What the hell?" he breathed, straining his eyes to see the minuscule font, which was obviously not meant to be seen. It was three little letters.

GTG

"Soul wasn't saying 'got to go'..." he realized suddenly. "He was telling me what to look for."

He hesitated momentarily, something inside him telling him not to proceed, then clicked on the small acronym. His monitor immediately turned black, and Xander wondered for a second if he had struck the off button. Then he saw it at the top of the screen. The link had opened up a kind of dos prompt within the site, and in very small letters read: PASSWORD PLEASE.

Xander grinned, resizing his browser window so that he could see his desktop, and clicking on a folder labeled *family photos*. When the folder opened there were no photos inside, just dozens of program icons. Some of them were of keys or padlocks while others had odd smiley faces or letters. One named *Devil's Advocate* had a cartoon image of the devil on it, and he right-clicked on it and clicked open. A new program window opened, the devil face in the upper left hand corner. He went back into his browser and copied the link for the password prompt he had gotten, then pasted it into the address bar of Devil's

Advocate and pressed enter.

The hourglass spun for a moment, then three words popped up underneath it and the devil's face turned to a frown: **NO PASSWORD FOUND.**

Growling under his breath, he closed out that program and opened up another, repeating the action. This time it was a smiley face that turned into a frown as the same words appeared on the screen.

He opened up a program with a key for an icon that he had created himself. The hourglass animation was replaced by one of a key turning in a lock, then after a moment the key broke. **PASSWORD NOT FOUND.**

One by one he tried with all his programs to figure out the password, but could not. He gave up, sliding a floppy disk into the drive and copying the site location onto it. Then he took the disk out of the computer and shut his bedroom door. He pulled back his dresser, revealing an old ventilation duct that wasn't used anymore. It was where he kept all the things he didn't want anyone else to find. He put the disk in there and pushed the shelf back into place.

He thought he heard a sound behind him, like the metallic clicking sound an old-fashioned clock made. He turned around fast. Pain again erupted from his right side when he was in mid-turn, sending him to the floor.

The pain was unbearable. He ground his teeth together against it, digging his fingernails deep into his carpet.

What the hell is this crap? he thought as he fought back tears. *It's like my side is on fire!*

Something inside him twitched and there was another burst of agony, stopping all coherent thought.

Struggling, his every move stiff and forced, Xander pulled himself into his bed. His muscles aching as if he'd just run a marathon, he rested for a moment and then quickly fell into a profoundly deep and dreamless sleep.

Carl Dent slipped silently past Mike's hospital bed, snagging some of his charts. He glanced up at the sleeping child, making sure he was in fact fast asleep, then turned and opened the file.

He looked them over quickly, jotting notes on what medication he was on and when he was getting out. His eyes widened a bit. They were letting the kid out next week.

"Gawd dammit," he cursed, biting his lip when he realized how loud he had said it, throwing another look at Mike to make sure he hadn't awoken the child. That didn't grant him much time.

Mike stirred.

Dent looked up momentarily, then quietly put the chart back in its rightful position. He looked at his pad with glee. It was Mike's social security number, birth date, and all other information. With it, he could find out exactly where Mike had been adopted from.

As he left the room, he saw a small security camera aimed directly at him. He realized quickly that he had no warrant to have invaded this boy's privacy. He reached up and unplugged the camera with one swift tug. No one could know. Frowning at his own actions he continued on, trying his best not to look back.

As Dent walked past the nurses' station, a tall nurse

with a pronounced upper lip and a nametag that read 'Riley' gave him a hard look as he hurried onto the elevator. As he got on, a man dressed all in black bumped into him while getting off.

"Watch it!" Dent stammered, his papers scattering.

The black man just walked by, barely noticing Dent was even there.

Dent hurried his papers together, then got on the elevator, muttering a long string of curses under his breath as he did.

The black man walked past the nurses' station and over to the room where Mike was staying. A room whose security camera happened to be offline. He took a piece of paper out from under his arm. It was the same one that Dent had been copying notes onto, his jot notes scrawled onto it in his almost illegible shorthand. He compared the number on Mike's door to the number on the paper and walked in. Smiling and as silent as the dead, he took an I.V. bag from inside his jacket and switched it with Mike's. He moved with such swiftness, as if every move he made was calculated, no movement made for no reason. The new liquid dripped down into the tube, then pumped itself into Mike's very veins, as the man slipped back out as quickly as he had come.

Dent walked down the street in a hurry. He wanted to get this information back to the station so that he could process it. Sweat began to bead on his forehead. It was unusually hot for this time of night. His bones began to ache as he walked faster and faster, accidentally dropping the stack of papers again.

"Fuck," he uttered, bending down to pick them up. A small pain was developing in his right side, but he ignored it. He had to catch the creep that was murdering these kids. As the pain only seemed to get worse the more he tried to ignore it, he mentally swore off Dunkin Donuts for the third time this week.

He heard a sound up ahead of him. He looked up, but saw nobody. The streets were deserted, an eerie quiet surrounding them. The type of quiet that was almost louder than sound itself could ever be.

The sound happened again, louder this time. Metal on metal.

Dent drew his weapon from its holster. *Maybe I won't need to track down the dirtbag,* he thought to himself, smirking a little. He put his back to the brick wall and slid on it to the corner, bringing his gun up to eye level. He swallowed hard and listened.

Several long moments passed, with no sound at all.

Then suddenly, a loud crash.

Dent spun around the corner and yelled "Police! Stop right there!"

The alley was dark and for a minute he thought the killer was hiding in the shadows, until he saw a small kitten crawl out of an old, dented garbage can. Dent sighed with relief, putting the gun back in its place. He turned to walk back toward the precinct.

He slammed face first into a large black figure. The person raised his long blade and drove it into Dent's side, jigging it up even further once it was in.

Dent shoved past the killer and broke into a run down

the street toward the station. Each breath caused his body to ache, every step making him want to bend over and throw up. He listened hard, hearing the click of the killer's boots as they stepped past the rocky path. They echoed loudly, the sound reverberating off all the buildings then back again, making it seem as though it was coming from all directions at once. He felt the blood run openly from his wound as he tried desperately to tap just a little more speed into his legs. Dent sped around a corner at top speed, finally ducking behind a doorway. He pulled out his weapon again, then looked through the door of the house he was standing in front of. It was deserted. There would be no aid there. He once again brought the gun up to eye level, peeking his head around the corner. Nothing. The street and all those connecting to it were completely void of all life. Dent once again breathed a sigh of relief as he lowered the weapon.

Smash. A great black gloved hand broke through the window of the house, grabbing Dent. He felt the broken glass rip at his flesh as he was pulled into the home.

He looked around and saw the corpses of an elderly couple sprawled onto the floor. Dent could tell that they had been dead a long time by the way the flesh was beginning to rot away, their icy cold gazes begging him for aid he could not give. Then Dent realized... *If they've been dead that long, this guy must've planned all this.*

Dent's eyes went wide as the killer stabbed once. Twice. Three times, then threw his now limp body to the floor. The killer put the weapon away, replacing it with a small scalpel. He bent over, stepping into the pool of fresh blood, letting the small, sharp knife cut through

Dent's tender stomach flesh, making a long line all the way down...

CHAPTER FOUR
SPIDER WEB

Sara Johnson was home alone that night. Her parents were over at Jamie Dawkins' house, helping his parents through this 'hard time'.

Why do people do that? she wondered silently. *They go over to comfort people they've barely spoken to before after a tragedy happens, to 'make things better', but they usually end up just making things worse. They remind these families of their loss, when these people should be getting into a routine to distract themselves from it. Some people think it best to face things like this. Sheyeah. Right.*

Sitting at her desk with her laptop in front of her, she ran a hand through her blonde hair, messing it into a tangled knot on one side. Taking a bite out of her Kit-Kat bar, she signed out of her e-mail account after deleting all the old messages from Jamie. The chocolate goodness gave her a slight lift that she had been in desperate need of and she couldn't help but smile as she took another nibble, brushing wafer crumbs off the breast of her shirt.

-BEEP- -BEEP- -BEEP- Sara's instant messenger called

out to her from her computer. She jiggled the mouse a bit to turn off sleep mode, then brought it down to the little yellow man in the corner of her screen.

"Spider?" she asked out loud, reading the name that popped up as the message's author. "Who the hell is Spider?"

She double clicked on the name to receive the instant message, and began to read it aloud. Her eyes went wide with fright and she backed away from the computer. She raced over to her door and locked it, then froze in mid-step and listened. From downstairs came the slow creek of footsteps.

"No way. It's just some moron screwing with me," she whispered to herself, then looked back at the screen.

I'm outside house.

She looked around the room carefully, her eyes darting every which way, searching for any sign of movement or life.

-BEEP-!

She jumped with fright, quickly putting her hand on her chest. With tears forming in her eyes, she went around to the computer and pressed enter.

Go to the window, came the new message, as cryptic and disturbing as the one before.

As salt water found its way down Sara's cheek, she made her way over to the window. The blinds were closed. She grabbed the swinging rope that would open them, closed her eyes, and took a deep breath. Biting her lip, she mustered up the strength to pull down on it, causing the venetian blinds to rise.

Stepping over to the window and looking down at the

ground below, she saw nothing. Leaning out, she turned her head to look out to the side of the driveway. Still, there was nothing.

She let out a long sigh, realizing she'd been holding her breath the entire time she was at the window.

"Sara!" the voice came suddenly as a head with scruffy dark brown hair popped out from the side of the window.

"Ah!" Sara let out a short yelp and held her chest as she realized who it was. "Xander! What are you doing here?"

"Good day to you too," he said cheerily, climbing in through the window as he wiped the sweat from his forehead.

"You jerk!" she yelled, slapping him playfully on the arm. "What are you doing here?"

"My parents went over to Jamie's too. I thought we could hang out a bit." He looked her over once, chuckling. "Have a small heart attack, why don't you?"

"Shut up! You would too if you got messages like that!"

"Messages?" Xander raised his eyebrows. "What messages?"

"Shut up!" Sara said. "You're always trying to scare me!"

"Usually yeah, but not this time, no."

They both stepped over to the computer and looked at the messages. "Are you telling me that isn't you?"

"Come on, you know my tag is Captain America. Besides, how could I have messaged this and gotten to your house in that amount of time? This is probably just some freak trying to scare you. It's just a cool coincidence that I came at the same time."

She nodded, acknowledging the impossibility of him sending those messages. She glanced down at the plastic bag in his hand, then looked up at him with a grin, her eyes both expectant and more than a little flirtatious. She did know him so well. "Movies?"

"Yup. One chick-flick, one for me, and a comedy for both."

"Should last us all night. What do you plan on doing in that amount of time?"

He smiled, blushing despite all his attempts not to. "I got *Sweet November* for you, *Apocalypse Now* for me, and *Big Daddy* for the required comedy."

"Let's pop 'em in," she laughed, as the two headed downstairs.

Nurse Riley was on duty early Thursday morning. It was only six o'clock and still quite dark out as she checked through all of the rooms to make sure everything was all right with the patients. She reached room 205 and looked down her charts. Harris, Mike. She glanced up at the unplugged security camera, sighed, then plugged it back in.

"Kids," she muttered.

She walked into the room and checked his vital signs.

"Well, you're doing better," she said. She looked at the charts from last night and compared them with the new signs. Her eyes went wide with shock.

"Oh! Way better!" She stepped out of the room for a moment. "Dr. Marx! Come take a look at this!"

A few hours later, Nurse Riley stripped the bandages off Mike as Cathy and both their parents stood and watched.

"...I can honestly say I've never seen anything like this," Dr. Marx attempted to explain, stuttering once. "He's almost made a complete recovery. I'm recommending him off the wheelchair and onto crutches immediately."

Marx was a stocky little man that looked like a cartoon mole, his lab coat hanging lopsided over a growing hunch on his back. Large rimmed glasses perched precariously on the edge of his nose and he adjusted them nervously as he spoke.

"That's great," Mike's father said, smiling at his son. He placed a hand on Mike's shoulder, as if to take his son's strength as a compliment to his own. "But how did this happen?"

"We're... uncertain, but we think that... actually, we have no idea what to think... but something, very strange, is going on here... ... yes," he said, looking over the reports as if to give validity to his response.

Cathy raised an eyebrow toward the older man. "Are all those technical terms why they pay you the big bucks?" she asked sarcastically, cuddling up close to Mike for the first time in days without fear of harming him.

"Yes... well..." Dr. Marx stammered again, attempting to explain again and then deciding it best not to even attempt to do so.

"Besides, who cares?" Cathy said, leaning over and kissing her boyfriend. "He's back with us, isn't that what matters?"

Mike smiled at her, touching her hair and pushing it back behind her ear.

She did have a way of putting things into perspective.

ᚨᚢᚨ

When Sara got up that morning, she threw the covers off herself playfully. She hopped out of bed with her nighty on (which was actually an oversized tee-shirt that had once belonged to Xander, featuring the Transformers symbol) then stepped into her walk-in closet to change into some clothes she didn't mind the world seeing.

She came out wearing a sleeveless shirt that read *0% Angel* across the chest and some slightly worn jeans that rode low in the front. She brushed a hand through her hair and made a small, disgusted grunt at how tangled it had become, then walked over to her dresser to get some socks, stopping to smile at the panda bear Xander had won for her at a fair. She gave it a little kiss, then walked over to the window to let the sun in.

Squish.

She looked down.

"Fuck," she said to herself, rising up her foot.

On the floor was a large muddy footprint. *Xander must have left it there when he came over last night. I'd better clean it up, or mom and dad might think I had a boy over.*

She laughed at her own little joke, then walked into the bathroom and grabbed a handful of paper towels. Getting down on her hands and knees, she began cleaning up the glob of foot-shaped mud. She brushed her hair back as she looked out the window over at Xander's bedroom.

She saw a little light go on, meaning his computer's alarm clock had just gone off. She smiled as she imagined him getting up and going through a similar ritual as she just had, wondering just how alike it actually was.

She finished cleaning the last of the mud and went to put the towels into the toilet for easy disposal. She dropped them in and was about to flush when she caught something out of the corner of her eye. She looked at the towels floating there for the first time since she had started cleaning. They were... red. She inhaled through her nose, and was immediately filled with the undeniable scent of copper.

The footprint had been made in blood.

She let out a little yelp as she realized what that implied.

"Sara?" her mother called out from downstairs. "Are you alright?"

"I'm fine, Mom!" she lied, running her hands over her head again and again, unsure of what to do.

"Come down for breakfast soon."

"Uh-huh!"

She stared at the red liquid on the paper towel for a moment. The blood was already seeping off of the paper into swirly rings around the top of the water, spinning around and making the entire bowl look dark red.

She quickly flushed the paper towel down the toilet, then walked silently back into her room. She looked out her window again and saw Xander at the computer. Suddenly, there was a loud -BEEP- behind her. She went over to check her instant message.

~CapTainaMeriCa~.

That was Xander. She couldn't talk to him right now. She clicked ignore, and began to think of *other* ways that Xander could have gotten blood on his shoe as she walked down the stairs to get breakfast.

The list was short.

"Ignore?" Xander read to himself as the little caption appeared on his screen. "Why would she ignore my message?"

He took a monster bite of the sausage that he was having for breakfast, then dipped the remaining morsel into a bit of mustard and popped it into his mouth, giving the screen a frustrated glare before closing it out.

He brought the mouse up to the left-hand corner of the screen and clicked on his bookmarks, scrolling down until he found engen.com.

He clicked on the little icon that represented engen. com and once again the animated symbol went through its cycle, only this time it ended with 'Stiff Upper Lip' by AC/DC. He quickly scrolled down the page and found the gtg icon and clicked on it. The dos password prompt overtook his screen again, the tiny cursor blinking next to the words PASSWORD PLEASE.

Wracking his brain and rubbing his eyes, which had veins like crow's feet from watching TV all night with Sara, he typed in Soul.

Password rejected.

Sighing, he typed in: Engen, and then Engen User.

Again, password rejected.

Groaning, he looked over on his desk and saw a newspaper. In it were the photographs of the alley where Jamie's body had been found, along with a story by Tom Drake and a one-column sidebar written by Don Smith. On the wall of the alley were those words again: 'Black Womb'. He glanced back at the computer, furrowing his forehead. It had the right number of characters.

The **password please** option came up on his screen again, and he typed in the letters: b - l - a - c - k - w - o - m - b and hit enter.

Immediately his screen became filled with image after image, windows popping up and then shutting themselves down before he could really see them. The screen began to flicker and he thought he was going to have a seizure. He strained his eyes against the brightness, trying to see at least *some* of the information before him. There was a headshot I.D. photo of a man with spiked hair and a devilish grin. Another showed an Asian woman with clear skin and tiny lips. A third showed what he thought was the street outside the Factory.

The more he watched the flickering images, the more pain began to build in his abdomen and at the base of his skull. Growling under his breath, he reopened the family photos folder and double clicked an image of a safe.

The images stopped flashing by, staying on the screen as the computer locked itself up. Not even the mouse would move.

"It worked," he said in astonishment, glancing over the page. "This shit looks... government."

He looked over the frozen window, seeing files on Jamie, Mike, even Cathy. Then he saw one that was marked classified. To him, that was an open invitation. He began to read down through this new information.

black womb, the. A project started through joint commission of governments to try to expand on the possibilities of genetic memory in stem-cell research. The end result would take decades, but would have eventually given way to a new age in foreign policy and sending men overseas. It would have been a super soldier. Although all tests failed to some degree, there was substantial increase in the field. The government project is currently owned by Owen McMasters, the lead research developer of the project, despite

The computer made a little noise. A caption came up that said 'location being tracked'.

"Fuck," Xander cursed, trying to regain control of the mouse and close out the program. The pointer stayed there no matter how much he jiggled it, as if it were paralyzed. Grunting angrily through gritted teeth, he held down the 'control' and 'alt' buttons on the keyboard then tapped 'delete' frantically.

At first nothing happened, the icon in the bottom right still spinning around and telling him he was being tracked.

Finally, the task manager popped up in the centre of the screen. He let out a sigh of relief as he ended all the programs one by one.

'Location being tracked' still dominated the bottom right of the screen.

Cursing again, he deleted the engen.com bookmark off of his desktop then pushed in on the computer's power button and held it until it was off.

He stared at the black screen for a long moment, resting his head against his hand as he leaned on his desk. He scooped up the last taste of mustard onto his finger and put it into his mouth.

"What the hell was that?" he asked himself, not surprised when he got no response.

Grendel flicked his pencil up at the ceiling, causing it to stick into the tile.

He wasn't interested in this biology lecture, not that he ever was. He was thinking about his party. With any luck, Mike wouldn't be able to make it. And even if he could, Sud, Tommy and Derek would take care of him. Either way, he'd finally get his crack at Cathy tomorrow night.

Tomorrow night.

It seemed so immediate and so far away all at the same time.

After Mike, the only problem would be that freak, Xander, and Sara. But they were easy enough to deal with. This weekend, he and Cathy would have his parents' house all to themselves...

"Julian!" Professor Miles slapped his hand down on Grendel's desk. His Boston accent was muddled by years in rural Maine but still very condescending and better-than-thou. A hail of pencils slipped from their places on the ceiling, crashing down onto Grendel's head. "Julian, you have not paid attention all class, your feet are on the desk... By god, you don't even have the right book!"

"But that's the book I've been using since the beginning of the year," Grendel objected, motioning toward it with both open palms.

The tired old teacher rubbed the bridge of his nose with his thumb and forefinger. "That... that actually doesn't shock me. I must be getting used to this." He took off his glasses and wiped them in his shirt, chuckling softly. "Dear lord, that is a scary thought, isn't it?"

"Can I use the bathroom?" Grendel asked.

Miles looked up, eyes wide in astonishment. "What?"

"Well, as Mr. Calendar once said 'better I am in the halls than in here bothering the students who want to learn.'"

"You are excused, Mr. Grendel."

Grendel hopped out from his desk and out the door as fast as he could, before Miles had a chance to change his mind.

He strutted up and down the halls of Coral Beach High as he'd often done before. The pale green lockers and tan walls were all very familiar to him, some even sparking fond memories. There was a spot between a row of lockers and the girl's rest room where he'd carved the anarchy symbol with a protractor late last year. It had been the only constructive use he had gotten out of the tool that semester. One of the lockers on his right still had a dent in it from where he had punched it after Greer had broken up with him.

He stopped at one classroom and looked into it.

There she was.

Cathy Kennessy, in all her grace and style. Her long hair shimmering in the morning light, her lips so juicy he could practically taste them... and he was convinced he could smell her specific aroma from where he stood.

She intoxicated him.

She spotted him outside, and smiled at him.

"Come out!" he mouthed silently, motioning toward himself with both hands.

She shook her head no, giggling.

"Come on!" he pretended to plead, bending down as if he were about to get onto his knees.

She relented, raising her hand.

"Yes, Miss Kennessy?" Mr. Calender said, pointing to Cathy.

"May I be excused? I kinda need to go to the little girls' room."

Calender smiled, motioning toward the door. "Go right ahead."

Cathy smiled, scooping up her book bag and heading for the door as the class resumed its discussion. She joined Grendel and the two of them began walking down the hall away from the classroom together.

"So, how's Mike?" Grendel asked Cathy in mock concern. Although he was looking at her, he was not even attempting to make eye contact with her as he asked.

"Fine. In fact, he'll be out this evening, so we'll both be at your party," she smiled, relishing in the news.

"Cool," he said, trying to sound overly enthusiastic about Mike's presence. *Looks like I'll be going with Plan 'B' then*, he thought to himself. "So what about Xander, is he..."

"Yup. In fact, I've been thinking about trying to fix him and Sara up," she said in a hushed tone, as if there were someone around to hear it.

"That'd be great. We should talk about that at the party."

"Sure," she said before she gave him a little hug and walked back to class. He watched her walk away intently, paying close attention to the slight swivel of her hips.

Tomorrow.

3:15.

Xander Drew got home from school and walked into his room. He went over to his computer, as usual, and jiggled the mouse.

Nothing.

"Oh yeah," he remembered, slapping himself in the forehead. "I had to turn it off."

He pressed the on button.

Still, nothing.

"What the hell?" he almost shouted.

He grabbed a screwdriver and opened up the tower, looking inside. The CPU was completely fried, melted to the rest of the machinery so bad that he wouldn't even be able to pry it off. It would take him weeks to replace, and that was if money was good.

"Damn," he sighed, tossing the screwdriver down and taking a chip out of the floor.

4:30.

"Frig!" Mike screamed at the little computerized character named Quartz on the screen as he let out a full force eye beam on his character, Ragna-Rock. Ragna went down easily, but then Diamond, the tag-team partner in this match, came out and started to lay it into Quartz. Diamond was the only female character in the game, and sparkled just like her namesake on the screen. She did a kiss attack, using her powers to sap Quartz's energy. It always reminded him of the effect that Cathy's kisses had on him, making him smile just that little bit more. Then, just as Mike was about to finish off Quartz 'HERE COMES A NEW CHALLENGER!' flashed across the screen in bright gold letters. He turned to see who had placed the money into the game, and smiled when he did. "Jerk. Why'd you do that?"

"Ah, you would've lost anyway," Xander replied, with Cathy and Sara behind him. "After the kiss attack, Diamond is really vulnerable to Quartz's punches and kicks."

Mike sighed. "How true. But I can still beat you."

"Right," Xander replied sarcastically, then took the opposing control stick and selected Granite and Obsidian to battle Mike's Diamond and Ragna-Rock. "I thought these guys didn't have any decent fighting games?"

"Came in yesterday," Mike answered absentmindedly, his tongue sticking out as he concentrated on the game.

Cathy and Sara took that as their cue that there would be no more attention paid to them for at least five minutes, both of them walking across the room.

"Boys will be boys," Cathy muttered to herself, sitting down on the racecar ride. The comedic cartoon announcer was taunting them from within the screen, telling them to 'race against ten other competitors for the world cup'. It was already beginning to get annoying.

"Yeah, but did you hear?"

"Hear what?"

"That secret service guy got killed last night, along with some old couple."

"No way," Cathy said, her eyes widening.

"Do you think the guy was right?" she whispered.

"What?" Cathy responded, astonished.

"About Xander doing it."

"No way! It's *Xander* we're talking about."

"Yeah, but if you did it, wouldn't you kill only the guy who thought you did it?"

Cathy acknowledged this. "Still. Sorry, Sara, it's just not in him."

Sara sighed. "You're right," she admitted, sounding less then sure.

ʎxʎ

"Autopsy report, Coral Beach Morgue. Thursday, the 22nd. Second report of this nature in three days. First of three victims, beginning autopsy now."

Harry Ford had lost his patented sense of humor. Some would call the jokes he made while dissecting the victims of horrendous acts of man disgusting. The truth was he had to joke just to keep from vomiting.

Lance Berkshire had a much stronger stomach, but a much softer heart. He handed the scalpel over to Harry, then realized it really wasn't necessary in the case of Carl Dent. His torso had a square hole cut into the centre of it, revealing cracked bones and a barrage of vital organs. "This time the killer took lungs, heart, intestinal tracks.... geez."

"Yeah, I know, Lance. I've been afraid to let my kids

outside the house at all, let alone at night." He took a small pause before returning to business. "Serial killer?"

"That'd be my best guess. I hear the police are exercising the possibility of gang and cult killings."

"God, what is wrong with this world," he murmured, but it wasn't a question so much as a general statement towards the plight of their town.

"It was definitely the same guy though. He took the lungs he didn't get the first time. Also the heart, small and large intestines..."

"Anything our creep hasn't got yet?"

"Well, muscle tissue, brain matter... he got kidneys and livers from the old couple..."

"Why? Wouldn't he want a younger one?"

"It appears our Mr. Dent had a bit of a drinking problem. But there's something even stranger."

"I'm almost afraid to ask."

"In every case, even that poor kid who wasn't killed... the appendixes were completely removed. But in the first case it was smooth, cut edges. Like one of us did it. This time... it's like it was done in anger."

6:00.

Dusk.

Tim parted two sections of his venetian blind and peered out into the street, making striped shadows across his face. The body count was now four, with a possibility of it rising within the next eight hours. He let the blinds fall back into place and paced back to his desk. On it were Carl Dent's files, both those he kept at the precinct and those found scattered near the murder scene. The only lead or suspect that actually made any sense at all was the Xander Drew file. A dark loner of a kid who hung around with the same people all of the time. It fit, but it wasn't enough to put anything on the kid. There were probably a hundred kids like that in this city. But then Dent went to that Grendel kid and that pushed the focus of this case in Dent's favor. *And now Dent's dead, but that may help the case, god forgive me for thinking it.* All they needed now was something solid. Some actual evidence...

"Sir?" the skinny blonde secretary called out, popping in her head from outside the door.

"Yes, Felicia. What is it?"

"There's a young girl here. I believe Carl Dent questioned her briefly in the hospital. She says she has some information which may be helpful. I think her name is Johnson."

"Send her in."

ʎ˅ʎ

Darkness covered Coral Beach that night. And when it came, the city closed its doors. Roadblocks were set up. Police were even borrowed from nearby towns to patrol the streets, which were like vacant lots, giving the entire town a ghostly tranquility. Everything was silent and still.

The only place still open was, naturally, the Factory.

The musicians had gone home and many of its workers wouldn't have stayed there for a million dollars, but the four owners and three of the customers still remained. Sud, Tommy and Derek.

Sud sat on the pool table opposite the one that Tommy and Derek were playing at. Derek leaned over the table and easily sank the eight ball into the corner pocket.

"Damn man. How'd you learn to play like that?" Tommy chided, shaking his head as he looked at the massive amount of balls he still had on the table.

"I just learned. That's all," Derek shrugged.

"You going to Gren's party tomorrow night?"

"Who isn't? Something tells me it's gonna be a wild time."

"Yeah," Sud grunted in agreement.

"Alright boys," Roxanne, one of the ladies that owned the Factory, called out from behind a desk. "We're closin' down. Pack it up and get out."

The three of them grabbed their coats from the rack and started out the door. They all lived in opposite directions. Derek was right across the street from the Factory, so they walked him to his door.

"You guys could come in a while if you wanted," Derek offered. "Call your 'rents, ask them to come and pick you up."

"Naw, man," Tommy shrugged. "We'll be fine."

Sud nodded in agreement.

"You sure?" Derek pushed, taking a quick glance around the street. "It's not safe out there, man."

Tommy just chuckled a little at that. "I don't think there's anybody stupid enough to try to take on us... not even lil' Xander Drew."

Sud laughed, but it seemed forced.

Derek smiled. "Yeah, I guess you're right. Take it easy, boys."

"You too," Tommy said, as the duo started walking home.

The street was cold. It wasn't winter yet by any means, but Tommy had noticed that ever since school started the temperature around town had become a fickle thing - warm one moment and then freezing cold the next.

The cold left an odd crispness on the street they walked on, like stepping into one of those walk-in freezers in the back of a restaurant. It sent sparks of life up through his calves and created swirls of dancing white mist that could only been seen in the direct light of the street lamps.

The rest of the street was covered in a sort of soft stillness. It felt like he imagined the inside of a snow globe would feel between shakes.

All of the storefronts were closed and the street was deserted, so much so that neither of them had ever seen the like before. Typically, Tommy found that every time he found himself noticing that the town was vacant, some car would pull out from behind a corner or some classmate would reveal himself from a doorway to prove him wrong. Tonight it was just the street... although the street itself seemed alive.

There was an energy to the street that came from the cold and the moon, that sort of electric vibrance that animated everything. The buildings seemed to loom high above the street lights until they were impossibly high and looking down on them. The houses they passed had dim lights in their windows and looked like jack-o-lanterns, their malformed and disfigured scowls glaring out at them.

Tommy pulled his shirt closer around him.

After a moment of silent walking he realized that it was up to him to initiate a conversation, because his near-mute partner never would. "Lookin' forward to the party?"

Sud nodded.

"Yea," he smirked. "I can't wait. It's gonna be a hell of a time. Julie told me she's gonna show, and Greer and Liz should too. Those girls..." He paused, throwing a smile at his compatriot. "Know how to party, if you catch my drift."

Again Sud nodded, this time adding a sly smile.

Then Tommy stopped.

Sud stopped too, more so to copy Tommy then for any other reason.

"You hear something?" Tommy said, swallowing hard.

"No. Why, did you?" Sud asked, his eyes starting to wander from side to side.

"Shh. Listen."

They did. And for a moment, there was nothing. Then it came.

-click-

Metal. The unmistakable sound of metal on metal sliced through the foggy air. They waited still.

-click-

Again, louder now, followed by a quick scuff like a boot or sneaker against the gravel. Sud and Tommy glanced at each other briefly, then broke into a run.

They crossed the street at the next intersection, ignoring the 'Don't walk' sign, then turned and ran up the next avenue toward Tommy's house. They could hear the metal scrape getting louder behind them. Louder and faster.

Whoever was following them was also picking up speed. Then Sud tripped, falling onto the sidewalk and scraping his knee.

"Fuck!" he yelped.

"Clumsy bastard!" Tommy yelled, stopping to help him up.

They looked back and he was there. A large, dark man looming over them, raising a long, curved blade. They both closed their eyes and prayed to god, waiting for the inevitable to happen... but it didn't. They opened their eyes and there was nobody there.

"Boys? You okay?" came a voice from behind them.

They both turned simultaneously to see Tim White standing by his patrol car about ten feet behind them.

They ran to him despite how their legs begging for them to stop, so fast that they slammed into the side of the car.

Tommy laid his head against the metal roof, sweat dripping from his nose and chin as he tried desperately to catch his breath in worn, wet gasps.

Sud fumbled with the door handle of the cruiser.

"Hey!" Tim protested.

"You gotta help us man, you gotta get us out of here!" Tommy cried, near literal tears.

Sud got in the car and just laid his head back on the cushion, trying hard to catch his breath. Tommy shoved him to one side and followed him in.

"Easy boys. It's okay now. You're safe," Tim said, trying to calm the boys. He turned around and looked at them, shaking his head.

Almost lost another two.

He turned the keys to start the engine. It started for a moment, then revved and went dead.

The boys looked at each other in the backseat. White looked up and down the street to make sure nobody was coming, then turned back to the boys with fire in his eyes.

"Get out," he told them flatly.

They looked at him oddly, then got out.

"Run. To the Factory. It shouldn't take us too long."

They obeyed and broke into a slow jog, trying to conserve their energy. But as they turned the first corner, Sud and Tommy both buckled over in pain.

"What?" Tim exclaimed, stopping to help them up. "What's wrong?"

"My... side," Tommy replied, clutching his right side and clenching his teeth.

"The appendix," Tim whispered, realizing something else all of the victims had in common. Even as the thought crossed his mind, he nearly fell over in pain himself, Sud catching him.

Tim glanced around nervously. "We've got to keep moving."

They began moving slowly through the streets on their way to the Factory. They crossed the next corner and it was in their sights, but the pain grew with each and every step. Sud had to ward off vomiting each time the heel of his shoe scratched against the cold pavement. Then, from behind them, came the sound that they had all knew was coming yet dreaded the arrival of.

-clink-

Metal, dragging against stone walkways. Then again:

-clink-. Much sharper this time than the last. When the sound happened again, Tim noticed that the gap was narrower then the first. *Whoever he is, he's running.*

They were on the home stretch now, running up the Factory's long driveway. They reached the door and began to thump on it loudly, trying to draw the attention of those inside.

"It's no use," Tommy sighed, motioning toward the driveway. "There's no cars. They've left."

"Damn," Tim muttered to himself. For a moment, all was quiet.

-clink-

They all glanced up in the direction that the sound had been coming from. Sud started banging on the door once more, followed by the others, this time in an effort to break it down. After a few moments, Tim motioned for the boys to stand back and gave the door a hard kick, knocking it off its hinges.

They entered. The lights were out, but the multiple arcade game screens created an eerie glow as their shadows flickered and danced on the wall. Tim made an effort to make the door look like it had been untouched, so that the killer might not suspect they had entered. Then, from behind them, they heard a loud thump. They all jumped around, staring into the gaping darkness.

"Roxanne?" Tommy called into the darkness. There was no response except for a sudden, sharp -clink-.

Tim pulled his gun out of its holster, stepping toward the entrance to the back room. He looked at the boys, then at the front door. "On three," he whispered.

They nodded.

"Three!"

The three of them bolted for the door and across to Derek's house. They looked behind them, seeing nothing. Derek's driveway was only a few feet away.

Tommy tripped on the sidewalk and fell to the ground, hitting the side of his face and drawing blood. White helped him up, looking around again. Nothing to be seen but cold, damp streets. They walked up to the front door and burst in. Derek's father came rushing in from the dining room, and Tim just held up his badge and tried to catch his breath.

Friday.

That was the first thought on Xander Drew's mind when he woke up the next morning. Every Friday was like a thousand years for him, with the boring drudgery of schoolwork to contend with. Each minute dragged on as if it were an hour and it was nearly impossible to get any work done because he couldn't stop thinking about the weekend if he had wanted to. More specifically, tonight. This was the night of Grendel's big party. It was to be (how did Sara put it?) the social event of the season.

The next thought to cross his mind was: *school*.

He brought his watch up to his face and pressed a button on its side, illuminating it in indigo light. The black numbers on the little screen read 8:50. The homeroom bell rang in five minutes. He jumped out of bed and pulled on a pair of tattered jeans, running down the stairs. His hair and skin were sticky, wet and more than a little warm. He made a mental note to take some of the covers off of his bed before he went to sleep tonight.

Halfway down he saw Sara, who was completely out of breath.

"School," she managed to stammer. Apparently she had slept in too.

"Yeah, I... Why didn't my computer's alarm clock wake me?" he thought out loud.

Sara stood up straight. "Yeah, mine didn't either."

They both pondered it for a moment, until Xander flicked on the hall light. Nothing happened. "Power's out."

Sara flicked the light off and on. "You're right. It's probably off at my place too."

Moreover, my CPU's fried, Xander remembered. *But I can't tell you that.*

They both thought about that a minute more, before they realized that they were already late for school. Xander grabbed his book bag and opened the door for Sara, then followed her out and started to run.

When she didn't run he stopped, figuring that she was tired from running to his house. She didn't say anything, merely nodding at him for waiting.

He motioned to put his arm around her, but she jerked away quickly.

He looked at her awkwardly for a minute, then started walking next to her. As they walked down the same road that they often had before, she noticed a growing pain in her side and bit her lip to steel herself against it.

She remembered that day, all those years ago. It was

her sixth birthday. When most little girls turn six they have a party with all their wild friends and eat cake until they puke, but not Cathy Kennessy. She spent her sixth grade birthday in an old, musty car with her parents driving to Coral Beach. It didn't matter to her where she was going at the time. All she knew was that all of her friends were back home in Pittsburgh and she was in the car. Because they were moving to a new place where her Daddy could get a job and make lots and lots of money.

They arrived at her new home at eight o'clock in the night and it was almost her bedtime. But she didn't have a bed yet, so she would have to sleep on a mattress on the cold floor.

From across the street came a little boy. He was about her height, his face covered in freckles. They looked at each other for a minute, almost wondering exactly what to think of one another.

The boy broke the silence. "Wanna play?"

She looked at him for a minute, then replied, "Okay. What's your name?"

"Michael David Harris. What's yours?"

"Cathy Elizabeth Kennessy. Do you know how to jump rope?"

"That's for girls..."

Cathy smiled at Mike from across the classroom. He winked at her briefly, then went back to finishing his question sheet. *Not exactly love at first sight*, she thought calmly as she went back to her own sheet. *But it'll do for a story our kids'll hear until they want to strangle us with it.*

Fourteen years old. That's when Sara Johnson thought it was all over. She was riding in the back seat of her boyfriend Justin's new car. He had just gotten his license and they were celebrating. In the car with her was Grendel in the back, and Cathy up front. She hadn't been dating Mike for very long then. They had just come from one of Derek's parties and Justin was about to bring them home, but he'd had a few too many drinks at the party. The car hit a bump in the road and started to swerve. The next thing she knew, she was being thrown from the car and onto the sidewalk. She didn't know how long she was out, but when she woke up there were red and blue lights flashing.

Police.

God, Mom is gonna kill me, she remembered thinking. That was when it struck her that she had almost died. She opened her eyes and there was a blurry image of a man looking down on her.

"Justin?" she murmured. Her eyes cleared and she saw the face she'd never forget. Xander Drew, her next door neighbour. She hadn't seen him much these last couple years; they'd drifted apart. But now, she jumped into his arms and cried on his shoulder.

Then she looked around. "Justin?"

That was when she saw it -- the limp body of her boyfriend being lifted onto a stretcher. There were cuts and bruises on his body everywhere and the chest of his shirt was soaked in blood. His eyes were open in an eerie gaze that sent chills down her spine. His hand fell limply over the side of his stretcher as they checked his pulse. The paramedic looked at his watch as his fingers pressed on the boy's neck. He shook his head and the two doctors put the white blanket over Justin's head.

She buried her head into Xander's shoulder and cried. He just held her. He didn't say a word, either from being in shock himself over seeing the body or just because he couldn't think of anything to say. Whatever the reason, he just held her for hours and hours. Long after the police, the paramedics and everyone else had left, he stayed there just holding her.

How could someone as sweet- Sara's thoughts were interrupted by Mr. Calendar raising his voice slightly in the middle of his sentence. Not out of anger, but more so to get the attention of the entire class. She looked up, slightly startled. *It just isn't possible.*

The voice of Principal Shnieder came over the intercom, which squealed a bit as it was turned on. "This is Principal Shnieder speaking. Due to the recent incidents in town, there will not be school until further notice. Also, a seven o'clock curfew has been placed on the town. Anyone caught out past seven will be brought home by a police escort immediately."

The announcement of school closing was followed by a barrage of hoots and hollers from students as they flooded out the doors. All except Cathy and Mike, who both realized what this meant: the killer had struck during the night.

CHAPTER FIVE
GOOD TIME

6:00

The party was just starting. Grendel didn't really want to start this early, but the curfew forced him to. It also ensured that once everyone got in, they had to stay until morning. Which was just fine for him, and one other person.

"School's out for summer!" Cathy and Xander chanted along with the music blaring over the speakers. "School's out forever!"

Grendel's front yard was packed with kids and it was hard for Mike, Cathy and Xander just to stay close to one another. Sara was over by Grendel, chatting away to him, although he didn't really notice. He was watching Cathy. Intently.

"This is a great party, Gren!" Tommy shouted over the speakers.

"What?" Grendel replied, putting a hand to his ear.

Tommy motioned for Grendel to speak in private. They walked away from the yard and into the kitchen.

"When are we doin' it?" he asked.

"Shh." Grendel put a finger up to his mouth and took a quick glance around. "You want everyone to hear? Alright, around seven o'clock, you, Sud and Derek ask Mike to help you lift something. You do whatever it takes to keep him out there. That's when I'll take Cathy upstairs to talk to her. If Xander starts being a problem, just dump him. Got it?"

"Yeah. What about Sara?"

"That fucking airhead slut? She won't be a big problem."

About forty minutes later, music still blared over the stereo. Everyone in the yard was bouncing and singing. Grendel's backyard was a large open space contained by high wooden fences stained a rich rusty colour that kept out prying eyes. There was a large brick barbeque a few feet from the north wall that was currently covered with speakers, and a metal fire pit near the centre that was clogged with cigarette butts.

The yard was filled with people attending the party.

From one end of the fence to the other, it was packed so tightly that it was hard to move, let alone dance, although people still managed. Drinks were passed from the cooler from person to person until they found their desired party. People jumped and swayed and pushed, turning the backyard into a giant mosh pit.

Jeffery Dunam made out with a girl a few years younger than him against the back wall of Grendel's house. He had a beer in one hand that was half empty, and was so drunk that every time he took a drink great splashes of it dribbled down over his chin.

Beverly Mass was throwing up into the barbeque, the roar of the speakers making her stomach do a back flip every time it urged.

Sara smiled, raising both her hands up into the air and bobbing along to the beat, bending her knees and thrusting her arms. "Whoo-hooo!"

Xander followed at her, watching the way every part of her danced. Her hair, her jacket... every part of her moved to the heavy bass beat. He smiled.

She turned and looked at him, both hands clenching his drink to his chest and his feet planted firmly to the grass.

Frowning and rolling her eyes, she slapped the drink out of his hands.

"H-hey!" he stammered.

"If it's not alcohol, it's not abuse," she stated in a factual tone. She reached over and grabbed both his hands.

His heart began to beat faster.

She raised their hands above their heads and pumped them, her fingers laced around his until he got the rhythm and started to do it on his own.

He smiled.

"You looked like one of the lawn gnomes," she said, pointing to a small cluster of little ceramic men that had been arranged in the corner so as not to get hurt. One of them was even holding a drink, in much the same way Xander had been. "It *had* to be corrected."

"Thanks," he beamed, continuing to pump his arms to the beat that Sara had started them on, even when the beat of the music changed. After a moment he started to bend his knees as well, trying his best to mimic her.

She laughed. "You're dancing like a girl."

He stopped, his already pink face becoming red.

"Here." She reached over and took his hips in her hands and started to show him how to move.

He could feel sweat trickle its way down his forehead. His throat became dry and his tongue refused to move.

"Move with it, first with one then the other," she said, biting her lip a little as she looked down at the way their hips pressed together, hers moving along with his. "Don't be afraid to lean into me. And don't over think it. Just... do it."

She looked up at him, meeting his gaze for a long moment.

She cleared her throat, then stepped away from him.

He continued to move, taking a breath for the first time in what felt like minutes.

"Yeah," she said, grabbing a cube of ice from the cooler and popping it between her lips. "That's better."

Around her the others continued to bump and grind.

ʌ⟨ʌ⟩

Cathy sat near the fire pit and watched Sara as she tried to teach Xander to dance, a wry smile finding its way onto her lips even as people pushed and shoved each other all around her. Calla McFadden's butt got dangerously close to hitting her in the back of the head every time she swayed to the music, but she tried her best to ignore it.

Mike appeared out of the labyrinth of bodies to her right, doing his best to avoid bumping into people as much as possible.

"Here," he said, handing her a drink in a red plastic glass. He had a similar one, which he took a long slurp from. "Virgin Jack and Coke, on the rocks."

"That's just Coke with ice," she laughed, taking just enough to wet her lips. "You sound like a douchebag."

He laughed, fizzling cola almost coming out his nose when he did. He brought his sleeve to stop it, the edges of his smile poking up over his arm. "I like it my way. Sounds important."

"What do you call an orange juice? A Virgin Screwdriver?"

"A Virgin Screwdriver is orange juice and 7Up," he said, raising an eyebrow at her.

"How do you know that?"

"How do you not know that?" he laughed, holding out a hand to her.

She rolled her eyes and took it, letting him help her to her feet. There was a short boy trying to dance with a rather tall girl in front of her, and she could see Sara and Xander again over his shoulder.

Xander was drinking his cola as though he were searching for the meaning of life at the bottom, wiping the sweat from his free hand onto his jeans as he did.

She shook her head at them and tisked.

Mike followed her gaze, then stepped into it to block her view of them. "You know in some cultures, that's considered rude."

"Stop it." She hummed playfully, bouncing on her heels to see over his shoulders and not even coming close. "I want to see."

"Yeah, I got that." He smiled. "Now stop it."

"Ugh," she huffed, folding her arms and puffing out her cheeks. "Men."

"Yes. Men get in the way of the picture show. Men drink of the beer and have of the women."

She glared at him, though she couldn't help herself from smiling. "Idiot."

Tommy hoisted his camera quickly and took a shot of Cathy, just as she was smiling at something Mike had said. He examined her image on the screen of his camera, its colour-corrected vibrancy making it look more real than in the dimming light of dusk. He'd caught her just beginning to laugh, in that wonderful and rare moment photographers called a Mona Lisa smile.

He clicked off a few more rounds in quick succession, examined the latest one on the screen again, then stepped back into the crowd.

He'd loved cameras ever since he could remember. He'd owned his first one at age four, and currently owned five. This one was a Canon digital-film hybrid with a facefinder feature he found remarkable.

He brought it to his face again, using the viewfinder to peruse the crowd.

John Walker was behind Calla McFadden, not so much dancing with her as he was holding her tight and swaying with her to the music. He was sucking on her collar and had left a long line of red blotches from her ear and down her neck before he had arrived there. Her bra was undone, one strap lying loosely over her shoulder.

-click!-

Tommy shifted focus, finding Sam Reynolds as she downed the last of a beer. Copious amounts of froth billowed down her cheeks on either side, fluffy and light like clouds.

"You're wasting some!" Wes King shouted next to her, pointing at her and pumping his fists radically. "Point goes to me!"

-click!-

Tommy turned and came face-to-face with Derek Smith, his boyish face and bushy eyebrows taking up the entire screen.

-click!-

"What the hell are you doing?" Derek frowned.

Tommy took the camera down from his face and smirked wide. "Documenting."

"Documenting what?"

"Everything," he replied, raising the camera high and snapping a random shot of the crowd. He examined the back of the camera and smiled, then turned to show Derek. "See?"

It captured half the yard, every face digitized and in perfect focus. The perspective was skewed, the picture taken while the lens had been tilted to the right and making everyone look like they were fighting gravity to stand on a deep slope.

"Not bad." Derek hummed, bobbing his head from side to side.

"Thank you," Tommy responded sharply, turning the camera back on Calla and John and snapping three quick shots.

-click click click!-

"Just don't aim that thing at me anymore, okay?" Derek grumbled, looking around. He saw Julie Peterson and smiled at her. She waved back.

"Why not?"

Derek turned back to him, his face serious for a moment, then grinned. "I've seen your room, with all the pictures around. I don't want you looking at me while you're stroking your moke."

"Fuck you," Tommy laughed, punching him in the arm.

Derek punched back, smirking so big that his earlobes moved. He nodded, then turned and started in the direction of the drink cooler.

Tommy turned and watched him go, then raised his camera and took another shot of him.

-click!-

Grendel stood on his balcony with his arms folded across his chest, nodding triumphantly at the amassed students. Sud sat next to him on a plastic lawn chair, his drink balanced precariously between his legs.

"This is what I wanted," Grendel said, stretching his arms out to encompass the yard. "This is what this class really needed! This party is going to go down in history!"

Sud grunted softly in response.

Grendel turned to look at him, his face drawn tight in a scowl so deep that the folds of his skin looked like cracks in the pavement after an earthquake. He shook his head, then squat down to be face-to-face with Tommy, who had his camera pressed to his face and was waiting for the opportune moment to snap a picture of Julie Peterson.

"What's his problem?" he asked, sticking his thumb over his shoulder at Sud.

"Liz Tyler kicked him in the balls after he got a little too grabby during the last song."

Grendel stood up and looked at Sud's drink, only now noticing that it was filled with ice and had no liquid in it whatsoever.

"Get up!" he barked, kicking the side of the chair and forcing Sud out of it. "You're supposed to be helping, not sitting there and licking your wounds like some --"

He stopped.

They all had, every person in attendance. Someone had even turned down the music as all eyes turned toward the orange-hued western sky.

The sun was starting to go down, and that meant one thing. Seven o'clock. They moved the party inside Grendel's house, where a lot of the first people grabbed couches to sit on.

Cathy snagged the love seat. Mike was about to sit down next to her, when a voice traveled over the crowd.

"Hey, Mike!" Sud called, unnecessarily loud. "Come help us with the speaker."

Mike's stomach turned.

You know that feeling in your side when you know something bad in going to happen? That sickness which ebbs its way up from your bowels and into your throat at the mere mention of a word? Right now, Mike was getting that feeling.

He turned and looked at Sud, Tommy and Derek from

across the hall.

"Sure. Just a sec," he drawled, then turned back and looked at Cathy, sitting on the love seat. He leaned over and kissed her lightly on the lips, then stood back up and looked at her.

"I'll be back in a sec." He smiled, then walked over to help Sud and the others.

Somehow he just had to say that. That feeling... the last time he gotten it, it had almost been the last time he had ever seen her. He put his hand to his side and squeezed his stitches a little, wincing in pain.

It's just the painkillers kicking in, he assured himself as he walked over and started to pick up a speaker.

Grendel's downstairs bathroom was a large step up from the Factory's, but it was still far from the Ritz.

It was a half-bath that his father used only to shit and shave in the morning, and was fairly utilitarian. There were no pictures or candles or decorative soaps. There was just a toilet and a sink, crammed in a space so small that most people wouldn't have used it for a closet.

Sara sat on the toilet with her arms hugging into her knees. Her jeans were down around her ankles but her underpants were still up, and the toilet lid was down. It was cold against the exposed flesh of her calves and made her shiver fiercely.

She was crying in big cartoon tears, praying that the music outside was loud enough to drown it out. Every so often she let out a wretched sob, some so powerful that they made her throat feel like it was being stabbed with a large knitting needle.

She'd come in to use the bathroom, but found that once the door was closed the urge had gone away and was replaced by this new one, which was much more powerful. She could have held her pee, she thought, but the water streaming down her bright red cheeks had come out like a tsunami. She wasn't even quite sure where it had come from. She hadn't been thinking about Jamie, at least not when she'd started. She hadn't been thinking about much at all. Now his image was frozen in front of her, like he was trapped in a bubble in her mind that she couldn't shake loose.

"Oh, God..." she wailed, although if anyone had heard it they wouldn't have recognized the words.

She reached down into the crumpled pockets of her jeans pocket with her thumb and forefinger. After a moment of fishing around, she withdrew a small blue tablet with an indentation on one side.

This time she pushed it past her lips with no reservations, swallowing it back with nothing but saliva. It hurt her throat going down, but then was gone.

Feeling better almost immediately, she pulled up her pants and examined her face in the mirror. Her eyeliner was miraculously still acceptable, but there were streaks slashed in the foundation on her cheeks that made her look striped. The flesh underneath was red and blotched. She sighed, then reached into her jeans again and withdrew her compact.

Mike let out a labored breath, his cheeks puffing out

comically.

"I think that's it for me, guys," he said, a smooth trail of sweat trickling down his face near his ear.

Sud looked over his shoulder and saw Cathy, still sitting alone.

"We're almost done. It won't be long now."

⋔⋔

"Hey Cathy," Grendel said, sitting down next to her in the love seat. "How you doin'?"

She giggled at him lightly.

He smiled at her.

⋔⋔

Sara was standing next to Joseph Townsend, laughing so hard at something he had said that she had to brace herself on the crook of his arm in order to keep herself up. She had a Coke in her other hand. It sloshed over the edges of the red plastic glass and her fingers with every giggle she made.

She wasn't standing far from the speakers, and had to lean in close to Joseph to hear him say anything. He smiled every time she got close, smelling the sweetness of her perfume that made his mouth fill with saliva.

A song by Linkin Park was playing on the stereo, and she was dancing in the barest sense of the word, bouncing on her knees and swaying her hips. She wasn't dancing to that song, though.

She was bouncing along to *Spirit in the Sky*.

Xander watched her from across the room, his own drink clutched tightly to his chest. He had yet to take a sip of it, and it had been sitting there for so long that all the fizz had gone out of it and turned it into stale sugar water. He took a deep breath, then turned around to face the wall.

"Hey Sara," he said sheepishly, fiddling with the curtain. "I don't know if you know this, but I'm-

"Stupid," he spat, forcing himself to let the fabric go. It fluttered back into place alongside the window and stayed there. "Hey Sara. I know you don't think of me like this, but I think that if you gave me a chance --

"No," he stopped again, rolling his eyes. "No, that's underselling yourself. 'Hey, this piece of meat is gangly and disgusting... buy it!' Stupid."

His throat was suddenly very dry. He took a long drink of his cola until he needed to draw breath. It was flat, and tasted like bile.

"Hey, Sara..." he started again, turning back toward the crowd. He almost bumped right into her. As it was, another great slosh of her drink splashed down onto the silver rings of her left hand.

"Hey, yourself," she smiled, steadying herself on her feet. "Enjoying the party?"

"Most definitely," Xander said enthusiastically.

She smiled at him.

He got lost in it for a moment, just staring at her. Her eyes were glossy, and he could see the brush strokes on her cheeks from where she had applied her makeup before going out.

She smiled at him again, nodding her head and waiting for him to speak.

"Oh!" he said finally, laughing humorlessly. "I had

something I wanted to talk to you about."

"Okay," she chirped, still bobbing along to the song in her head. "Anything in particular?"

"Yes," he said. "No. Maybe."

"Glad we cleared that up."

"It's not any one thing. It's... look, we've know each other a long time, and --"

"Hey! You dropped one! You gotta take a shot!" she howled at someone from across the room, pointing at them wildly with her drink hand. She was still laughing when she turned back to him. "Sorry."

"That's okay."

"What were you saying?"

"Yes. What I was saying. What I was saying was -"

"This is the end of this year's flute hanger!" someone called from the next room.

Sara laughed, so hard that she almost fell over onto Xander.

"Hey, listen, you wanna go talk?" he asked, smiling as she helped herself back to her feet. "This place is a little loud."

"Yeah, sure."

He motioned toward the curtains he'd been playing with. When he pulled on the drawstring next to them, they opened and revealed a sliding glass door that lead out onto the balcony.

"Sly," she said, tossing him a playful wink. "If I didn't know better, I'd have thought you planned this."

Xander laughed.

The two of them walked out onto Grendel's balcony. The cool night air whipped at them, her light blonde hair blowing gracefully backward, exposing her neck and chest. He found himself looking at her unintentionally.

"Dear God, you're beautiful," he said finally, with the honesty of a person who had been waiting forever to say it.

She smiled at him, with those beautiful lips that she had painted sparkling platinum for the occasion. "Excuse me?"

"I said you're beautiful," he repeated, turning to look her square in the eye.

"Yeah," she laughed. "I got that. But why?"

"Because," he said, taking her hand. "You are."

He leaned in to kiss her. She looked up at him, moving in slightly herself, her lip quivering in an anticipation she hadn't even realized she had had until now. Her eyes fluttered back and forth between his lips to his eyes and his did the same, making eye contact every so often. He could smell her perfume and it overwhelmed him. He could feel the softness of her body, so close to his and yet still not touching. Slowly, they moved closer together. Closer...

"Xander," came a voice from inside.

"What?" Xander turned, angrily.

"We need you for something in here." It was Dave Marston, a jock friend of Jamie's. "It's this weird thing with Gren's computer. Some kinda net nanny keeping us off. You wanna...."

"Yeah. Just... gimmie a minute."

"Alright."

Xander looked at Sara for a long moment, smiling. "Hold that thought."

᠕᠊᠊᠕

"Dammit," Grendel muttered to himself.

"What?" Cathy asked.

"I just remembered. I still didn't find that Ragnarok CD."

"The one with *Old Maid in Alaska* on it?"

"Yeah."

"Darn," she whined. "That's my favorite."

"You wanna go look for it?"

"Alright."

᠕᠊᠊᠕

Xander was busy at the cluttered computer. The keyboard was literally covered in papers.

"Geez, doesn't he know how to take care of it? He's got homework from last month on here, gum wrappers ... even his new Ragnarok CD..."

᠕᠊᠊᠕

Mike and Sud dropped the stereo to the floor when they were half way to the door.

Mike stretched and wiped the sweat from his brow. "Sorry I can't help more guys. My side still hurts."

"S'alright," replied Derek.

Mike glanced over into the house. Cathy wasn't on the love seat anymore. She was going upstairs with Grendel. "Hey!" he shouted, but then fell to the ground as Derek punched him in the side.

The *right* side.

He could feel a stitch split as he went down onto his

knees.

"What'd ya?" he started, then got kicked in the ribs by Tommy.

"Nothing personal," Sud said in his stupid tone. He walked over and punched Mike in the back of the neck, sending him down for the count.

᛭

"It can't be here," Cathy said, lifting pillows and blankets around on Grendel's unmade bed trying to find the CD.

"I'm pretty sure it is," Grendel said as he looked around, hardly taking his eyes off Cathy.

"I'll go down and check the CD rack." She sighed as she walked over to the door and twisted the knob.

Nothing.

"It's locked," she said in a much lower tone. "Why would it be locked, Gren?"

She looked over at him.

"No way," Grendel shrugged. "Let me see."

He twisted the knob himself and got the same result. "Geez. How'd that happen?"

He turned to face her and she looked at him for a second, her eyes narrowing as she figured out what was going on. He put his hands on her hips and leaned in to kiss her. She jerked away.

"What the hell are you doing?" she screamed.

"Hey, don't be like that." He put his arms around her.

"Grendel, stop it!" She struggled against him, but he was much stronger than she was. He pushed her down onto his bed and got on top of her, kissing her forcibly.

"No!" she screamed.

He put his hand down onto her leg, the spot where she had been slashed. She winced, and he took the opportunity to begin to take off her shirt...

"See? It's really very easy to get into Windows from dos mode," Xander explained to the computer illiterate that had gathered around him. "All you have to do is type in 'win' and Windows should automatically start up, unless there's something wrong with..."

"Grendel, no!" came a cry from upstairs. He'd have recognized that voice anywhere. There was something wrong with her. It was Cathy and there was something wrong with her.

"Cathy?" Xander shouted up the stairs, jumping away from the computer. "Cathy!? Are you alright? Grendel?"

He began to wander toward the stairs, picking up speed as he went.

"Hold it," came a voice from behind him. He turned with a start and came face to face with Tommy.

"What's going on? Where's Mike?" Xander asked, staring him down. He knew something had to be wrong. He was getting that same feeling in his gut that Mike had had, but it was elating, overpowering everything else. It made his pulse quicken and his blood boil.

"Grendel, please stop..." came Cathy's voice from upstairs again. This time it had become obvious that she was crying, and what Grendel was doing to her.

"I think you ought to leave those two alone," Tommy

said, giving Xander a little push.

Xander looked around, seeing the increasing amount of people gathering around. They were all staring at Xander, their brows furrowed.

Tommy folded his arms as more screams and sounds of a struggle came from upstairs.

Xander looked up the remaining stairs, then back at the people who had begun to move in on him. He broke out into an all out run for Grendel's room and made it to the top of the stairs before Sud grabbed his pant leg, causing him to tumble and fall.

The crowd parted as Xander rolled down the stairs, landing with a thump at the bottom. The crowd formed a little circle around him and he tried to get up, but Derek kicked him in the side.

There was a loud, wet snap that Xander recognized as the breaking of a rib. His left hand went immediately to his side while the other propped him up until someone stepped on it, creating an ear-shattering crack. Xander grunted in pain and he could feel tears forming in his eyes. Somebody else from the circle punched down onto his neck and he felt blood rise up into his throat. It left a coppery taste he'd always hated. He looked up, blood smearing down his face and onto the floor.

"All you had to do was nothing," Tommy scowled down at him, his arms folded.

"Go to hell," he said bluntly, the sound of his voice muffled by the blood in his mouth.

Tommy gave Xander a hard kick, knocking his head back onto a coffee table, where he finally lost consciousness.

"Grendel, please..." Cathy pleaded. He already had her shirt off and now he had her jeans unbuttoned. "Please, just stop."

"Shh. It'll be alright," he said, kissing her forcefully, pushing her shoulders onto the bed.

Tears ran down her soft, freckled cheeks. She sobbed and he stopped for a moment. He looked down at her, then slowly starting to pull down her jeans. But of course to do that, he had to let go of her with one hand, which meant that she had one hand free. She wracked her nails against his face, leaving four large scratch marks.

"Ow!" he exclaimed, putting his other hand up to his face.

She was free now, but the door was still locked. She ran over to the window, trying desperately to open it.

"You stupid bitch!" he shouted, punching her across the face.

She hit the floor like a ton of bricks and then started to cry once more.

"I'll teach you..." he slapped her across the face.

Through her tears she looked around the room for something, *anything* she could use as a weapon. Something to defend herself with. He sat on her and grabbed at her. In desperation, she kicked him in the groin.

He bent over in pain, then drew back and punched her again. Then he got up and tossed her clothes onto her. "Pff. You're not worth the trouble. Stupid whore."

He kicked her once as hard as he could, in the ribs, then left. He went back down to his friends to lie, to tell them what the two of them had done.

She was still crying uncontrollably. There were already bruises starting to form on her face and chest. As she got up and got dressed, she happened to glance in the mirror at her battered face and her puffy eyes. She broke into a whiny cry and walked out into the hall. When she got there, she started to feel dizzy. Her head started to hurt and then, without warning, she lost consciousness.

Grendel was greeted with the hoots and hollers of his friends as he walked down his stairwell. The music started to play again and everyone got back to the party. Grendel walked over to Tommy.

"Did the guys give you any trouble?" he asked, grabbing a drink from an end table and taking a long slurp.

"Naw, take a look for yourself." Tommy laughed, cocking his head in the general direction of the downstairs bedroom. In it, Mike and Xander lay sprawled across each other. Their faces were masks of pain as they slept off their injuries.

Grendel walked over and closed the door. "We'll have some fun with them later."

Outside, Sara was still waiting for Xander to come back. She had no idea what was going on inside the house. Out here, everything was quiet. She stood there, her head hanging over the balcony, her satin shirt swaying in the breeze behind her. She looked out at the lights of Coral Beach, sparkling along with the stars in the sky. On a night like tonight, it was hard to tell where sky ended and the earth began. Everything was quiet, still, peaceful... perfect. She closed her eyes, took a deep breath of the cool night air, thought of Xander, and felt a smile cross her lips.

-Shink-

She opened her eyes.

-Shink-

Again. A metalish sound, like Mr. Calendar desperately trying to create a spark with two pieces of metal in the physics lab.

-Shink-

Again. This time she looked around.

Nothing.

Just the cool air and the black of night.

Fidgeting and rubbing her exposed arms, she turned to look around.

There was patio furniture on the far side of the balcony, of the sort that was typically hidden from public view unless it became very necessary to have it out. It had been painted white with some sort of base that didn't agree with it and the colour chipped off in random shapes, revealing rust underneath. The vinyl strips that covered the chairs were broken in places and missing in others, creating a mishmash hammock of plastic and metal that was sure to leave its user nervous and uncomfortable.

There was a book bag sitting snugly in the lap of the chair closest to her. The plastic buckle on it had drooped down over the side and swaying lightly into the breeze, connecting with the leg every so often.

-clink-

-clink-

-clink-

She sighed, then placed the buckle onto the chair and went back to looking out onto the city.

-Shink-

She sighed again, turning to put the belt buckle back on the chair.

It hadn't moved.

-Shink-

She looked up, leaning over the rail of the balcony to see if there was anyone under her. Suddenly, there was a sharp pain in her side. Blood oozed into her shirt as the killer twisted, then pulled the knife from the mouth it had just opened. Sara let out a little sound like a dove cooing, a small tear rolling down her cheek. The killer wiped her cheek clean, then sliced her slowly across the throat. Her hand went up to her wound, and was instantly covered in blood.

The killer put a finger up to his hooded mouth. "Shh."

She opened her mouth to scream a warning to the others, but couldn't. All she felt was her blood pour out onto the wooden balcony. She lay down on the floor and her eyes rolled back into her head as a small puddle of blood began to form all around her. As the killer walked through it, he gazed into the room filled with teens. A wry smile spread across his lips.

The last thought to go through her mind was of Xander.

༺✿༻

Tommy sang drunkenly on the coffee table, a small group of people incoherently singing along with him.

"need to rewind myself..." Then without warning, he fell onto those gathered around him. Swears were loudly uttered by those directly in his path, but then they all started laughing. All but Tommy. He was clutching his side violently. Eventually, the laughter stopped and all eyes were on him. "...pain..."

The power went out in the house, plunging it into darkness. The music stopped playing and everyone was still.

Sud walked over to the front door and tried to open it. "It's jammed," he said.

Everyone looked at one another and around the room cautiously.

"Hold on... hold on..." Grendel mumbled as he fumbled through a junk drawer. "Geez, a fuckin' power out and all you guys turn to pansies." He pulled out an old phone book, grabbing an aged flashlight under it. "Here we go."

He turned it around for a moment before finding the switch, then turned it on. Nothing. There were a few disappointed moans from the crowd. Grendel frowned, tapping the flashlight against his palm twice. A beam of light cut through the dense darkness. "There."

He swirled the light around. What the beam found made him feel sick.

Hanging by a rope from the ceiling fan was the body of Sara Johnson. Her once vibrant and beautiful face was caked with blood. Her clothes were in shreds, barely covering her. There was a gaping hole in her right side, some of her major organs were visible. Her hands were in twisted, deformed positions, like claws. Her hair (formerly soft and lovely), which had been put up into a bun for the party, had been let down. It was matted in blood, giving it an eerie, brittle look.

One girl screamed in the crowd. However for the most part, people just stared in a silent shock as the corpse swung slightly on its rope. The slight breeze in the room made her spin just a little. Grendel looked up into her eyes. They stared blankly back at him, fixed on nothing. They used to contain light and life, but now had a smoky, glossed over look to them. He felt his lower lip begin to tremble.

Suddenly pain ripped up and down his right side. The flashlight dropped to the floor with a clunk and he strained his neck to look behind him.

The dark spectre behind him twisted the knife in its wound before pulling it from Grendel's entire body. He took the long knife to Grendel's back, driving it through until it protruded from his chest cavity.

As Grendel dropped to the floor with a thump, people in the room began to scream and run hysterically. The man threw his knife, digging it into a young girl's back. He looked down at the flashlight on the ground, stomping his foot down onto it and immersing the house in total darkness.

As darkness enveloped the crowded living room, many people kept running and screaming, but one young girl stayed statuesque and still. Frozen in the shock of seeing friends killed before her very eyes or just having absolutely no idea what to do. Or maybe it was that she had come to the conclusion that there was absolutely nothing she *could* do. Whatever the case, this one girl, no older then fifteen, just sat there curled into a little ball as others pushed past her in an attempt to find an exit. She looked up from her fetal position and stared blankly into the darkness around her. She let out a long breath, the first she had taken since the house had been plunged into blackness. The breath followed the darkness' movements through the cold air before it eventually became one with it.

It's funny what goes through your mind during intense situations. All of a sudden, she realized that she had missed the latest episode of *Survivor* last night. She remembered that the Toronto Maple Leafs and the New Jersey Devils were even now playing against one another. That she had an exam next week in World History, that she had forgotten to walk the dog before leaving her house and even that she had left her television on. All of these things and more wandered through the girl's head as she stared into the total darkness surrounding her body.

Something flashed before her eyes.

She glanced about nervously, struggling to stop the sobbing that might give away her position. The moonlight shone in through the broken glass window, creating eerie silhouettes as her friends realized that there was nowhere to run and settled on hiding. There was a dead silence looming in the air.

-thunk -

The sound of a friend's body dropping to the floor after a quick, silent death.

-thunk-

-thunk-

-thunk-

Over and over again. The girl turned her head to the floor, attempting to pretend that she was a piece of furniture. The hardwood near her reflected the moon's light up into her face, as the wood was slowly enveloped by a different kind of darkness. A dark liquid rolled, and then streamed over the floor, eventually cascading lightly onto the girl's sneaker. She continued staring down at it. As the moonlight reached it, the liquid took on a reddish tint.

Blood.

Suddenly, all the thoughts which had previously clouded the girls mind were erased, replaced by one word that continued to scream within the depths of her mind. *Blood. Blood. Blood...*

She looked up into the darkness again, and again she sensed movement within it. Abruptly, the moonlight caught hold of something else: a long, metal blade. Before she could react in defense or even scream, it was upon her.

She felt the blade slice clean across her throat.

She attempted to let out a cry but heard no sound despite all efforts. The killer's strike had destroyed her vocal cords. She put a hand to her neck to try and halt the blood which now flowed freely. She knew this kind of blow rendered the victim dead within seconds, so she strained her neck so that she could look her destroyer in the eye. She fully expected him to finish her, deliver a killing blow across her head, but the blow never came. Instead the slayer just stood there, watching as the girl clung to life by a thin thread, her blood staining the floor and mixing with that already there.

After a second that seemed to be an hour, she lost strength and collapsed to the floor, her skull landing on the wood with a loud crack. The killer cracked a sinister smile.

〱〱

John Walker crawled slowly along the edge of the wall, trying to stay out of the path of any light. He crept along, as silent as humanly possible, attempting to get to the shattered glass the murderer had entered through. He reluctantly stepped on a shattered piece, the quiet crinkling sound it made echoing through the dark room. He stopped and looked into the darkness to see if his position had been realized, then came to the fruition that if he had been he would have to move even faster and kept going.

-thunk-

A sound from the darkness that he recognized, yet wished that he hadn't.

-thunk-

Again.

-thunk-

-thunk-

He kept going, his eyes beginning to get hazy from tears of knowing exactly what was happening in the darkness. He looked ahead and saw that the window was only a few feet away. Letting out a short, raspy gasp of excitement before becoming silent again, he listened to the sounds in the darkness.

There was some soft sobbing, followed by a slinking sound and a sharp crack.

He moved forward again, but realized that he would not be able to step over the glass without blocking light and attracting attention. He would have to crawl over it. Lifting his two hands over first, he began to pull himself along. The jagged, toothed glass stuck up from the doorframe, cutting into his abdomen as he made his way along. Blood ran freely as the sharp glass ripped and rendered the tender flesh of his chest and stomach. He bit back a yelp of pain as a piece of flesh got stuck on a small, razor-like piece of glass.

Rather than go back, he moved forward, pulling on the piece of hanging flesh. It stretched momentarily, before the glass itself broke off into the wound. With the stomach out of the way, John now stepped over the glass with one foot, lifting it high to make sure what happened to his mid-section did not happen to more sensitive areas. He lifted his other foot over in the same fashion and began a slow crawl over to the edge of the balcony where he would jump the two stories to freedom.

Suddenly, he felt a tug.

For a moment he thought that the killer had finally caught up with him. He stayed perfectly still, almost waiting for the inevitable to rain down upon him. But it didn't. He turned his head slightly, enough to see that his jeans were hooked on the glass. He turned back for a second, giving a short sigh of relief. Believing he was out of trouble, he pulled his leg forward. Riiiiiiiip. The sound of fabric tearing cut through the air like a knife, and John knew that there was no chance the killer hadn't heard it.

He stopped, listening to the darkness again.

There was a dead silence, and he thought for sure

that he was finished. Then he heard the sickly reassuring sound of his redemption.

-thunk-

The sound of yet another friend's body dropping to the floor. He sighed again. The fact that he was relieved, almost happy at the sound of death made him want to vomit. He sucked it back and pulled his leg forward again. His jeans pulled on the glass again, this time causing it to break. As if in slow motion, the glass flipped and spun as it cut through the air before landing on the ground and shattering with a clink that cut through the muteness. All at once it seemed as though the previous quiet had been nothing. It was as if even the silence had shut up.

It finally came to John that he had been discovered. He got up quickly, running to the edge of the balcony. He paused only for a moment, staring into the darkness behind him. Hearing the loud, heavy footsteps of his stalker behind him, John saw the glint of his blade as it swung from side to side in his back holster. He turned his eyes back to the ground below and, placing a hand over his stomach wound, jumped over to it.

His loss of blood and the couple of Budweisers that he'd had all gave him the sensation of flying, when in fact he was only falling. He didn't even do that for very long. He felt an enormous pressure on his throat as his downward momentum came to a halt, and he had a brief sensation of weightlessness.

The killer had grabbed his collar.

Throwing him onto the balcony, the killer let loose with a hard kick to the ribs. John bent over in pain as he rolled through the glass and back into the house, almost exactly where he had begun. The murderer loomed over him, the moonlit night casting the shadow of him down upon his latest victim.

He took the drawstring from a window shade and held it up to the light. There was a warning on it that advised that children could choke on it. That sinisterly evil smile once again curved his lips, showing his sharp teeth. He wrapped the string around the chandelier, then around John's neck. He picked John up with both hands and held him up for a moment, supporting his weight.

Then, smiling, he let go.

There was a loud crack as the string went taut against John's neck.

Another girl attempted to run for the exit and the killer threw his blade into her back, sending her toppling to the floor.

He twisted the blade before ripping it out with a sickening sucking noise. Bringing the blade to his thick lips, he licked some of the blood off, then wiped the rest away with his index finger.

ᚲᚷ

Frightened and scared, Liz Tyler wandered from room to room trying to find one that had been left open. She could hear the sounds from the living room with crystal clarity. -thunk-, -thunk-, -thunk-, -thunk-, a weird cracking sound, followed by a loud rip and a lot of footsteps.

She tried one door after another in an attempt to escape the inevitable peril that was crashing down onto her like a wave onto the shore. Grendel's bedroom door had been barred shut, as had been the downstairs bathroom.

Her only option left was the spare room. She rushed to it quickly, reaching out her long, slender arm and turning the cold metal knob.

To her immense relief, it turned freely.

She swung the door open and almost closed it again with fright. Before her were Cathy and Mike, laid down on each other, both unconscious. She stepped back for a moment. Then, hearing a wet snap in the living room she stepped in, she closed the door and locked it behind her.

She glanced around the room, and finally just curled up in a corner and started to sob as water ran down her cheeks.

She was only there a moment when she came to a realization: *Wasn't Xander supposed to have been in the room as well?*

The killer looked around at his handiwork and smiled, then walked from the living room into the hallway. He kicked down one door and looked inside.

Nothing.

The next, a bathroom. Nobody inside.

Then he found his way to the spare room.

Forcing the door open, he stepped inside...

Liz heard the latch on the door break. The door swung open and slammed against the wall. She buried her head into her arms and pretended that she was invisible. She was breathing hard, her chest near convulsing. When the killer came into view, she felt her heart skip a beat. He walked over to Mike and Cathy. He turned Cathy onto her back so that he could see her face. He held it in his hand for a moment before he heard it. Heard her. He turned and stared down at her, shaking in the corner. He reached down and picked her up by the scruff of her neck, then reached to his back to draw out his sword... then stopped when he heard a new sound.

The sound of police coming.

Some concerned neighbor must have called the police.

The killer looked down at his prey for a moment before he merely threw her against the wall as if she were a rag doll, snapping her neck. He opened the large bay window and stepped out, taking his leave.

CHAPTER SIX
ZONE

Mike awoke on a stretcher. He opened his eyes then immediately closed them again, forcing them to adjust to the light. He opened them a second time, this time as he got up.

A paramedic rushed over to him. His name was Richard Dreyfus, and less than two hours ago he had asked his girlfriend of two years, Marjorie, to marry him. She'd said yes, and they'd both cried happily. Her three-year-old son had thought something was wrong at first, and had patted Richard soothingly on the back. It had been adorable. They'd all laughed, and he'd given the boy a hearty kiss on the cheek. The idea of being his father was overwhelming and good, and he hoped the feeling would never go away.

His pager had gone off just as Marjorie was calling her mother.

It seemed like a lifetime ago now.

"Easy, son," Richard said, putting Mike's arm around his shoulder. "You'll be alright if you just sit down and rest. It's over now."

"W-wha?" Mike stumbled, having trouble getting the word out. His head felt like it was in a vice. He put his hand up to it, only to discover a rather thick layer of bandages surrounding it. Suddenly, his eyes went wide. "Cathy?"

"She's fine. Would you like to see her?"

Mike nodded, and the Richard helped him to his feet and around the corner of the ambulance he had been sitting in the shadow of.

There were cars parked all over the front of Grendel's front lawn, and the lawn next door. Police cars and ghost cars and ambulances, all of them flashing their lights in different patterns and casting a stuttering red hue over everything in their path. It was like the streets had been painted in blood, and as he looked beyond this street and onto the next, he saw that it continued out into the rest of Coral Beach. Maybe even the entire world.

There were bodies lined on the grass. They didn't look like bodies, covered in zipped-up black bags that looked like the ones Mike's father took his suits to the dry cleaners in. It didn't help, though. He knew what they were, lined up seemingly forever and casting long, thin shadows with the light.

Police and paramedics and firefighters scrambled everywhere. They ran around and past each other, one somehow never hitting the other. Some people stood and just surveyed the chaos. People cried. There were more sirens far away, as well as a constant buzz of radios as reports were updated and then re-updated.

Cathy was sitting on the sidewalk with a blanket

wrapped around her shoulders, her head enveloped in her arms. She looked up at the sound of approaching footsteps.

"Mike." She smiled, wiping tears from her eyes. "They wouldn't let me see you until you woke, and--"

"Shhh," he said, placing his arm around her. "It's alright now."

She broke down crying in his arms. "No. It isn't. It never will be again."

"What do you mean?" he demanded in a hushed voice. "What's happened?"

"It's Sara..."

⋏⟨⋏

Rumors spread like a wildfire in a small town like Coral Beach. By the time Monday morning came and the exact number of the dead had been counted, that wildfire had turned into a forest fire. Especially with Xander Drew among the missing. The worst part was all of the rumors came back to Mike and Cathy.

"Now I'm sorry I have to ask you two these questions," Tim White said to Cathy and Mike from behind his desk. "I understand that you've been through a lot and if you want to do this later, that'll be fine. But I want to catch this killer."

Cathy looked at Mike.

"Now will be fine," she answered for the both of them.

"Alright," he opened his folder with a sigh. "I know this is a sensitive issue for you, but do you think... it could have been Drew?"

"Xander?!" Mike exclaimed. "No way! Never. Not in a million years. No."

Tim raised his hands in surrender. "I know it's hard, but there is substantial evidence now. The three of you were locked in that room, according to your own statements, right?"

"Yes," Mike nodded.

"Now, this killer shows up, starts murdering everyone that Xander always hated and now your boy is gone. Not only that, but the first one he killed was a girl who had turned him down repeatedly."

Cathy wiped her eyes at the mention of Sara.

"Then, the killer comes across you two. You were his friends, which is why he overlooked you. Which is why you were some of the only survivors. Then, he leaves. He realizes that he's outsmarted himself and that people like me would put two and two together, and he runs. And now he's out on the streets somewhere."

Cathy was crying.

Mike looked at her, then turned back to Tim with hatred in his eyes. "Okay. That's your opinion. Here's what I think happened. This killer is just another freak serial killer in a long, sad line of freak serial killers. He kills for a reason, but one that we don't fully understand yet. Anyway, before he tried to kill Tommy and Sud the other night, he heard them talking about Grendel's big party and decided to crash it. That's why he let them get away, when he probably could've killed both them and you. So, he shows up at the party and kills a lot of us. That girl, Liz you said... right? Well, she runs into the room where Xander, Cathy and I are being kept. He follows, but thinks that the three of us are already dead, when we're really just unconscious. He kills the girl and the sound wakes up Xander. So, the killer saw Xander wake and was about to kill him, when... he hears the police approaching. Rather than leave his plan undone, with no time to kill Xander in the grotesque and elaborate ways that he employs, the killer decides to take Xander with him if only for a little while. And yes, the killer is on the streets somewhere."

Tim looked thoughtful, leaning back and stroking the edges of his mouth and chin.

"That's what you think happened, huh?" he said calmly.

"That's what I know happened!" Mike shouted in response.

"Mike," Cathy said, speaking finally. She turned to Tim with a look of desperation in her eyes. "Xander didn't do it. And if he ran... you can be sure it was for a good reason."

"What reason would that be?" Tim pried, fingering his pen against the paper.

Cathy looked away, staring instead at the wall in an effort to fight back tears.

"He didn't," Mike said again, tapping a finger against the desk to elaborate.

Tim looked taken aback, then he restored himself. "Okay, son. You can go."

Mike got up, taking Cathy by the hand. "Come on, love. It's over now."

They left Tim that day with much to think about, and much to reconsider.

He bent over his desk and looked at the massive pile

of files in front of him, one for each person killed during the ordeal. Jamie Dawkins. Carl Dent. That elderly couple, the Jacobies. Liz Taylor. And at least thirty other teens from Coral Beach High, including Julian Grendel.

Of all of them, Xander was their only link... except for the Jacobies.

He furrowed his brow.

"Maybe..." he thought out loud, pulling the file on the Jacobies forward. "I'm playing this the wrong way. Stop looking for what they all have in common... and look at the one that doesn't have anything in common..."

He opened the file. There was nothing there. There was the autopsy, but that was it. No birth record, no death certificate, no fingerprints, no dental or medical records... nothing.

"What the hell...." he mumbled, pushing through page after page of blank documents until he found one with something written on it. It was a copy of Salvadore Jacobies' record of employment, of which there was only one position for which he had reference.

"What the fuck is Engen?"

"Coral Beach Precinct Morgue. Tuesday, the 26th. Harry Ford, mortician for this evening."

The words were once an attempt at levity and humor. Now, as they were delivered with a sad voice muffled by sobs, they just served to add to the weight of the situation.

"Come on, Harry," Lance said to his partner through tear filled eyes. "We've got a job to do."

Lance's wife had always asked how he could do this job. How he could *dissect* the bodies of his fellow human beings, even if it was in the pursuit of whatever killed them. He had always replied that there were worse jobs out there. That police and firemen often had to deal with gore *and* danger on the job. That stunt artists in movie crews lost partners on the job in grotesque ways all of the time. But right now he could not think of a single job worse than his as he stared at the thirty freezer drawers, each one containing the body of a child under the age of twenty. He fought back tears. "Come on."

He pulled a white mask over his face and asked Harry for a scalpel, then pulled back the blanket covering the chest of the first patient and began to cut into the chest cavity.

⋏⟨⟩⋏

"Where could he be?" Cathy said to Mike.

They were in Xander's room, which was a total mess as usual. Cathy sat on his bed, where she often had before while Xander downloaded music for her. She'd always thought of this space as warm and inviting. Now it was just cold and empty without his presence.

Mike paced about, looking for anything that might lead him to Xander's whereabouts.

Xander's mother had let them go up, but had refused to go herself. She hadn't been able to since she heard the news of his disappearance. His shirts littered the floor around his bed and his pants were strung across a chair at his desk. The drawers had been taken out of his dresser and thrown onto the floor. The room had been ransacked almost beyond recognition.

"Who would do this?"

Mike was repeatedly flicking the power switch of Xander's computer on and off, with no result.

Did this happen to the computer before, or did whoever broke in do it? he thought to himself. "Uh, I don't know. But I can take a guess."

"The killer," she said softly, a shiver running down her spine.

"He must have been looking for something. If he wasn't, he probably would have killed Mr. and Mrs. Drew," Mike continued. "The question is: did he find it?"

"I don't know. But we've got to figure it out good and fast before that cop jumps to any more conclusions."

"Well," Mike muttered as he pushed aside an old bookcase. "If I know Xander, if he had something important to hide, he'd put it here." He stepped aside, revealing the ventilation duct to her. He pulled the grate off of it and reached in. His hand came out, first clutching a bundle of adult magazines.

Cathy rolled her eyes in disgust.

"I'm pretty sure that's not it," he chuckled.

"Duh. Unless our sicko is a major, um, sicko."

Mike reached in again, this time coming out with a little disk marked: ENGEN.

"What is it?" she asked, snatching it away.

"Dunno," he replied, snatching it back. He held it up to his eye. "But I'm sure as hell gonna find out."

Nothing.

And more nothing.

It seemed as though no matter what Tim did, there was nothing linking the Jacobies to existence. It was as if they had simply appeared dead in that house, out of thin air.

There was no record of them in any state, or even any country for that matter, that he could think to search. It was like they were phantom bodies.

This is it, he thought to himself, hunched over his laptop computer. *This is what I need; this is what's different. One of these things is not like the other and this is definitely it. If only I could figure out what 'it' was.*

The only thing he had to go on was the name Engen, which he could only assume was a business, but there were no records of it. Anywhere. Ever. It was like it too simply existed on that one slip of paper and nowhere else.

He let out a heaving sigh and felt the uncontrollable urge to pick up smoking again, something he hadn't done since he was a kid. His parents had told him that those things would kill him. Obviously they hadn't grown up in Coral Beach, or they'd have realized that the cigarettes would just have to wait in line for the chance.

He closed his eyes tight, realizing suddenly that he hadn't slept since Carl was killed.

When he opened them, he was looking directly at Carl's desk across the room, next to the window.

His brow crumpled as he looked up, something sparking in his mind and then fading again.

"Now what was that thought I just had..." he asked, almost begging his mind to let it return. He clicked his tongue against the roof of his mouth, staring at Carl's desk. "What are you trying to tell me, old friend?"

He sighed.

His fingers started to dance over the keyboard, as if they had a mind of their own. He went onto the national adoption agency and typed in both of the Jacobies.

No less than fifty hits came up with children they had adopted going back forty years or more, in almost every state and a few in Canada.

"Curiouser and curiouser..." he mumbled, scrolling down through the list.

Coral Beach High School Library.

They could feel the eyes on them. Somewhere in the back of their minds, they could sense it.

However, Mike and Cathy couldn't really care less right now, as they popped the disk marked ENGEN into the school's computer.

There was a little internet browser file labeled engen. com. Mike looked at it for a second, then brought the cursor up to it and clicked. Instantly, the browser popped up and began dialing in the name engen.com. When it did come up, the site was blank.

"This is what was so important?" Cathy wondered out loud.

"No. They've fixed it so that nobody will find out what was on that site," he said, then pulled the disk out of the computer and looked at it. "Whoever they are."

"Thirty-nine bodies done, one to go," Lance said

aloud, with a miniature sigh of relief.

"Yeah, sigh now," Harry muttered, pointing a finger at the list of corpses. "But our murderer friend has changed his M. O. No organs were missing from any of these victims. Tim White's not gonna like hearing that this may have actually been a copycat killer."

"You're wrong. This last victim," he pointed to number forty on the sheet. "She was ravaged. She had her ovaries and the rest of her reproductive system taken."

Harry looked down through his sheets. "Sara Johnson. What's so special about her?"

⋏⟨⋏

"Tim?" the secretary said as she poked her head through his doorway.

Tim removed his reading glasses. "Yes, Felicia?"

"Those two children you saw earlier are here again. They say that they have some new evidence..."

"By all means, send them in," he smiled, turning off his computer screen.

Mike and Cathy walked in. Mike looked stern. He didn't like White. At all. He threw the disk onto his desk. "Have you ever been to engen.com, Mr. White?"

⋏⟨⋏

New entry. We have waited nearly twenty years, but our boy has finally returned to us. Restarting test for the darkness. Black Womb is home...

CHAPTER SEVEN
ENGEN

"AAARRRGHHH!" Xander screamed in pain, arching his back and pulling against the safety harnesses placed all around his body.

He could feel what they were doing, could feel them inside of him. If he turned the right way at the right time, he might even catch a glimpse of one of the doctors or the shadow of a guard. It barely registered with him. He was in too much pain to really register anything else. He screamed again, feeling a pinch deep inside his body. *Why are they doing this to me?* was all he could think. He had done nothing wrong. He hadn't hurt anybody, or anything. The last thing he remembered was actually trying to help someone. His friend, Cathy...

He screamed again. This time, finally, he got a reaction.

"Doctor?" the female shouted from somewhere above. She sounded muddled and dulled at first, as though she were under water, then came into clarity and was so loud that it was all he could hear. His vision was blurred and there were a lot of bright lights in his face, every so often something moving between him and them. "Can't we do something? He's in pain for god's sake!"

"No!" a male voice exclaimed. "Now, I don't like it any more then you do, but we can't put him to sleep because it'll dull his reactions. We can't administer an aesthetic to him because that'll affect..."

"Carry on," came a harsh voice from over an intercom. There was an audible click as it turned on and off.

"Right away, sir. Nurse, do something about his screaming."

A shadow fell in front of the light. The nurse bent over him, wrapping thick cloth around his mouth. He mumbled against it for a moment, then tried to scream again as the doctor went back in. They'd been at it for hours. The worst part was remembering every detail. He had been strapped down to this steel bed, his arms and legs stretched outward. He remembered the doctor telling him that everything would be all right, then asking the nurse for a scalpel. He cut right across Xander's stomach, pulling the skin away and holding it there with metal clamps. He was routinely given drugs to prevent him from blanking out from pain. He could feel the blood slowly pumping out of him, only to be replaced by even more. He felt the doctor pushing organs from side to side, looking for something. His arms and legs had been cut to stop him from struggling against the restraints. He did anyway. That pain was of little consequence in comparison. He turned his head and watched the blood trickle down the side of the table, the metallic buckles on his stirrups glistened in the intense light coming from above. He fought against the straps once more, then gave off a long sigh and gave up.

Suddenly, the doctor pinched something that made his whole body convulse without control. Xander clenched his teeth until the intense pain ceased. He was watching the doctor pull something long and yellow from him when the nurse came over and shone a miniature flashlight into his eyes. She whispered something to him. He was too out of it from anguish to actually hear the words, but the woman's calm tone soothed him. Until the doctor went back to work.

"Nurse, get away from there," the doctor said sternly. "Sponge."

An assistant handed the doctor the requested sponge, which was used to wipe some splattered blood from his brow. The assistant then faded back in the darkness that surrounded the operating table.

New entry. Tests continue. The patient has exhibited the same resistance that his mother used to employ. This slows the testing process and inevitably causes the subject great pain. A most unfortunate waste of time.

Xander cried out in torment once again. The noise was ear splitting, and would have chilled normal men to the marrow. The doctor never so much as flinched. He cut away the last part of the rib cage, his eyes getting wide. "Dear sweet mother of god..." he uttered.

"What?" the nurse reacted in fear. She looked over the

doctor's shoulder and saw what had frightened this cold, hard, emotionless man so much.

Blackness. Where Xander's appendix *should* have been, there was instead a cancerous blackness. It didn't look to be attached to the appendix organ at all, but more like... *replacing* it. The doctor regained his composure. He had been briefed about all of this, but had never actually expected to find it. Never in his life would he have thought such a thing could exist.

The blackness convulsed in synch with Xander's pulse, as if it acted as a secondary heart of some kind. It had gray spots which were lumpy, unlike the jet black areas which appeared to be smooth and almost silky. Valves protruded from the blackness to other areas of the body.

It's spreading, thought the doctor.

Acting fast, he pushed the darkness aside with a gloved hand to reveal: more blackness. It had touched many major organs. The heart had tiny speckles on it. The liver was a sickly gray on one corner. One lung had been completely enveloped, while the other remained untouched. It seemed that it had even *dissolved* some of the bone structure of the rib cage, feeding off the marrow. Not only that, but the thing seemed to be beating faster now. The doctor could see where darkness was being pumped through his body at a faster rate.

"It's spreading faster," the doctor said, sounding extremely worried. "We'll have to amputate."

"NO!" came the voice over the loudspeaker again. "I will not allow it!"

"Too bad! We've waited almost twenty years for the subject to return, and I'm not going to lose him again now!"

The doctor raised the scalpel.

All this time, Xander had been screaming like a banshee. Now, seemingly for no reason, he just... stopped.

Curious, the nurse walked over to again check the boy's eyes. She immediately dropped her little flashlight. Placing her hand over her mouth, she screamed. "His... his eyes!"

The doctor rushed over. Xander's pupils seemed to have completely taken over his eye, as they were now entirely blackened in, taking on a glossy appearance.

"It's spread to the optical nerves," he announced, going back to the blackness. He raised his scalpel once more and drove it into the dark substance.

Or at least, he attempted to.

The darkness resisted, acting sort of rubbery, bobbing whenever the doctor poked at it. Finally, he decided to cut the valves surrounding it and take it out whole. He cut a small slit in the top valve. Dark liquid spewed out onto his scalpel and hand, pulling on him. He screamed. It burned at him, scalding the flesh. The darkness was still being pumped onto him. It was sticky like tar and it seemed that the more the doctor pulled away, the more it held. The nurses and assistants crowded around. Two strong looking guards took the doctor around the waist and began to pull. With a loud snap, the doctor finally got his hand back. The flesh had been stripped away, revealing bundles of nerves, and muscle. He cried out in agony, falling to the floor and passing out. All eyes were on Xander, when something amazing happened.

From the slits made in his wrists and near his ankles,

black liquid began to bubble and squirt. It first covered his hands and feet, then slowly it moved its way up his skin like waves move on a shore. Xander began to expel the substance from his mouth and within moments he was vomiting it upward, allowing it to flow back down onto him. As it did, his muscles seemed to grow exponentially, expanding as the substance touched it. His skin gained a smooth, yet scaly and shiny texture, like cohesive gel. He screamed, but all that came was the gurgle of the liquid. The experience was obviously painful. The gaps closed at his chest. He was now completely covered in the black liquid.

Three red slits formed on his face, opening to reveal two triangular bright red eyes and a glowing red mouth. Slowly, turquoise liquid filled the red of his eyes until that was all there was, making them look like pools of swamp water. The creature that was once Xander Drew broke the bonds which restrained it and stood up, much to the horror of the onlookers. It then said something in a deep, scratchy voice:

"Black Womb lives."

The creature leaped onto them, grabbing the doctor by the throat and squeezing. Blood ran from the neck down the monster's arms, but it hardly even noticed. Its eyes shone brightly in the dimly lit area surrounding the examination table. The Black Womb looked down onto it with disgust, throwing the doctor atop it. Tools and instruments flew everywhere and the scalpel which had been previously used against Xander Drew now made its final mark, digging into the chest of the doctor.

Black Womb turned its head to the assistants and

nurses, who were clambering toward the exits. When it turned, its face turned first. Its face turned and then its head, something that paralyzed the nurse with fear.

There was a man outside of the door, engulfed in the shadows of the coat he wore. Only the bottom half of his face was visible, and was drawn upward in a smile. He looked down and turned something, then held up a key for the assistants to see. They began to scream angrily at the dark-suited man.

He laughed.

The creature looked at the men and women as they beat on the shiny metal door with panicked fists, swearing and uttering threats to the dark-suited man. Then they stopped and turned to Black Womb, who had not moved an inch after killing the doctor. It crouched on the steel floor, staring at the people. One by one, they all turned and locked into its eyes. Those eyes reminded one woman of a cat's eyes as it watched its prey, following them wherever they went.

It began to stand up now, as silent as a breeze, every movement without effort. As it did, it opened its mouth, revealing two rows of thick, jagged teeth. It held its hand up to the light and a look of concentration came over its face. Suddenly, four black talons unsheathed, one from each of its fingers. It crouched again, ready to pounce on the people who now stood perfectly still. A long, slender forked tongue protruded from its mouth and licked its lips before retreating. Without warning the beast pounced upward onto a wall, only long enough to kick off of it, propelling itself into an assistant. It drew back its arm, which now appeared long and elastic, pointing its clawed fingers at the man's face.

There was a slight hesitation in its posture, as the moment seemed to hang in the air. Then, with unbelievable speed, the creature slashed down across the man's face, tearing at his tender facial skin. It stuck one of its claws in its mouth and sucked a bit of blood off. The creature smiled sinisterly as the medical assistant clutched his burning face, screaming loudly. His screams were followed by those of the other workers as they realized what had happened to their fallen partner.

It sprung at them again, this time landing a few feet in front of its female target. It clenched its hand into a fist and punched her in the side of the head. She flew across the room, smashing her head against the concrete wall, leaving a trail of blood in her wake.

He turned his attention to a third victim. This one was male, somewhere in his early twenties, and was slightly overweight.

Black Womb jumped onto him. Pressing against the man's chest with his feet, it forced him forward into a wall. It wrapped its hands around to the back of the man's head, inserted its claws into his skull and *pulled*.

Looking around at the dead bodies of all the medical assistants, the creature was satisfied that it had slaughtered them all... until he heard it.

The soft rhythmic whimpering, like the gentle coo of a pigeon on a warm summer's day.

Then the monster remembered the nurse. It walked over to the metallic table that had once held the doctor's tools, flipping it aside. There, curled into a little ball, was the nurse. Her blonde hair was matted over her face, her eyes peering from between the strands in cold fright.

It looked at her and appeared sympathetic. She looked up into its aqua eyes, and seemed almost... comforted. It sheathed its claws and extended its hand, gently brushing a stray piece of hair from her face to behind her ear. Then its eyes suddenly took on an evil, triangular slant. It grabbed her head and forced it to the side, exposing her slender neck. Opening its mouth wide, it bit down on the tender flesh. Blood flowed freely as the second row of teeth sliced through her jugular vein. It sucked in hard, drinking the life giving liquid. The nurse attempted to scream in pain, but her throat had been too damaged in the attack. Her body convulsed. It grabbed her to stop it, then finally flung her aside, hurling her against the wall. It growled long and loud, tossing its blood soaked head up toward the ceiling.

The metal door slid open, and the black suited man stepped into the room. The door hissed to a close behind him. He walked over to Black Womb and smiled.

Black Womb turned its head to one side and started to claw at its own face in pain as red liquid pumped and swirled its way into its eyes. The aqua colouring was forced out, melding and conforming to the new colour with a sickening squish, looking like dye placed in water as it churned about. It took a deep breath, looking around as if confused.

Inside of it, Xander Drew gasped. He looked around at the bodies surrounding him then up at the killer standing before him, his eyes widening with fear and his mouth going slack. The Womb's face on the outside mimicked the motion, but it looked more like a hungry animal spotting a slab of meat, its mouth salivating when he opened it.

How did I get here? Xander thought feverishly, looking down at his hands and seeing the claws for the first time. *What the hell is this?*

He tried to remember how he even got off the operating table and how all these people had died. As he stared at the body of the young blonde nurse, he felt a sick memory come over him, then forgot it instantly. It reminded him of when he tried to access corrupt files on his computer. They would try to open, then fail. An ache from his head made him think that if he tried too hard, his brain might lock up.

He looked up at the killer, hatred in his glowing eyes. "You killed Jamie."

The murderer nodded silently.

"Who are you?" he demanded in the Black Womb's voice, struggling to get the words out, as if training its own throat how to utter each new syllable. The corners of his eyes began to glow aqua, then returned to red.

The killer threw away his hat and whipped off his trench coat, revealing a skintight jumpsuit. The suit was black and leather, with pointy white triangles showing along the waist and shoulders. There were two blades crossing at his back, each one double sided, curved and glinting in the dim light. The killer removed one of the blades, gripping the rubber handles. He flipped the blade in his fingers, then held it in place diagonally at his side. When he finally spoke, the words were cold and unforgiving. In a voice sick and raspy, he said:

"Call me Genblade."

CHAPTER EIGHT
GENBLADE

"Call me Genblade."

The words hung in the air for a moment. Xander looked up into the dark eyes of the killer, staring silently into his inner soul. He saw nothing but a blackness that rivaled even his own. There was a deep pain building in his side and he could feel the Black Womb's heart convulse wildly, fighting against the rib cage.

Genblade took out a small device, pressing his thumb against the switch.

"Waddaya know. This thing really does detect the Darkness," he chuckled, throwing it onto the floor next to them. "This shouldn't take too long." He was confident, and rightfully so. His muscles bulged against the black spandex as they tightened and shifted.

Then Xander realized why.

Genblade leaped almost five feet into the air from a standing position and flipped over his opponent, landing on the other side and slashing at the Womb's backside. Blackness spiraled in long slithering strands in the direction of the blade, the wounded human flesh underneath visible through the gap in the oil. The slashed strands slithered their way back, rejoining Black Womb at the hand. Within seconds the wound had closed and was followed by the gap in the blackness closing up as the strands flowed back into place.

The Womb stood up and tilted its head to one side until the calcium popped, then turned to face its attacker. "No. It shouldn't."

Genblade gritted his teeth. His eyes narrowed into little slits on either side of his pointed nose and his fingers stretched along the grip of his sword. The blade hung by his side loosely until he let it fall until it almost hit the floor, then caught it. Extending his arm slightly, he let the metal touch against the metal of the tile, creating a small sound.

-shink-

-shink-. Again.

He did it over and over, all the while keeping his eyes locked on the Black Womb's opaque pupils. The Womb stared back at Genblade, but with each -shink- the urge not to look down at the blade became unbearable. It strained, forcing itself not to comply with its reflexes. Genblade paused for a moment, the blade rising as he finished scraping the floor.

-shunk-.

Genblade had let the blade drop again. It created a louder, more intense scratch. The Womb's pupil moved down to the corner of its eye as it glanced, only briefly, at the blade. When it looked back up, Genblade was already bearing down upon it. The spiked blade ripped across

Black Womb's face, briefly revealing the guise of Xander Drew underneath, writhing in agony.

Black Womb reeled backward in pain, gripping at its face with its hands. It howled as it remembered the claws too late, ripping them away and taking a large chunk of its own cheek with it. The sliver of meat dropped from the talon as it retracted and fell to the floor with a plop.

"Gah!" it hissed, staggering as it tried to steady itself on its feet.

As the brute's arms flailed, Genblade kicked it in the side and sent it teetering even more off balance. More specifically, its *right* side. The creature's mouth opened wide as it forced back a scream of pain. It looked up at its opponent standing over it, as it crashed to the ground.

Inside it, Xander's pulse began to beat so loud that it was all he could hear thumping at the base of his skull.

I'm done, he thought, gasping for air and getting a mouthful of the dark bile that covered him instead. *I may have power, but I have no idea what I'm doing. This guy has skill. He knows what he's doing and I don't. He's better than me.* He growled as he got up again, clutching at his side. *Don't know what's going on, but if I've got power I've got to use it now. Use so much of it that it won't matter how hard this guy's trained himself. None of it matters. I've got to get out of here, Cathy still needs me.*

The Womb raised its hands, palms open. It gritted its teeth as its talons unsheathed from their holding places inside of its fingers again, each one accompanied by a tiny spurt of arterial blood. It lunged at Genblade, mouth open and arms reaching out toward the murderer, aching to repay him for the flesh it had lost.

Genblade shifted his weight to the right foot casually, letting the Womb pass harmlessly by.

"This is really starting to get sad," he tisked, reaching out and grabbing the creature by the back of the throat. Bringing him up to eye level, Genblade looked at the monster and laughed, slamming its head into the hard metal floor, then raising it up again.

"Guh... tit... gug," the Womb mumbled as both red and black blood spewed from its lips, its head bobbing around on its neck as if one of the joints which held it there had come loose.

"You know what the difference is between you and me?" Genblade taunted, forcing it to crash into the floor once more, then bringing it back to eye level again.

Black Womb merely stared at his assaulter in a cold response. Xander's bruised and cut face was visible through the small gap in the oily substance, before it swallowed into itself.

"No, not about a hundred I.Q. points," he quipped, smashing his rival into the now bending metal once again, then brought it up to answer the question himself. "It's just like I whispered to that dumb blonde before I cut her."

Xander's eyes went as wide as they could while still bruised, and the Womb's followed.

"You can knock 'em down, drive skates through their hearts or shoot 'em, but one thing always stays the same."

SLAM.

"...death ALWAYS has a face."

SLAM.

"ALWAYS has a name."

SLAM.

"And today, that name is Genblade."

SLAM.

Genblade looked at his adversary for the first time since beginning his little speech. The Black Womb's healing process had obviously slowed, the blackness now looking as though it were painted on and barely clinging to the flesh beneath. About half of Xander's face was visible now, and it was in bad shape. The wounds looked to be closing, but not as fast as before. His vision was impaired by large, swollen bruises and his cheek and forehead were cut deep with gashes.

Xander's pupil turned to look at Genblade, his voice somewhere in between the Black Womb and his own. "Sara?"

"Bit the dirt like a starving earthworm."

SLAM.

SLAM.

SLAM.

Suddenly, Black Womb's eyes began to glow bright aqua again. It reached behind itself, grabbing Genblade by the wrist and digging the claws in deep to hold it there. With a quick pull of his arm, Black Womb flipped Genblade over its back, slamming him onto the blood stained floor. Black strands flew off of the Womb everywhere, healing his wounds quickly. It picked Genblade up by the neck and pushed him against the cold metal wall.

Blood ran from Genblade's nose, flowing down his chin. He smiled, licking his lips of the red liquid.

"There you are. Was wondering when you'd come back out to play," he teased.

Black Womb stared at Genblade, looking as if it wanted to say something. It opened its mouth to speak, but nothing came. After a moment it managed three words, each one sounding as though it were vomited up rather than spoken. "Black Womb lives!"

"Had a feeling you were going to say that," Genblade snickered as he started to rise to his feet.

The Womb grabbed him by the shoulder and threw him straight across the room as if he were a rag doll. He slammed into another wall, smacking into a light hanging from the ceiling as he went. The light swung around for a moment, making shadows dance and jump everywhere. It blinked several times from the impact, creating a strobe effect and made it hard to focus on anything in the room. It couldn't even focus on Genblade or where he was in the room, or even on its own hands.

When the light finally flickered out, Black Womb stared into the darkness and saw nothing. It put its clawed hands in front of it, preparing for the moment that Genblade came out of the shadows.

Suddenly, it felt an extreme rush of pain in its right side. It looked down and to its shock, he saw the end of Genblade's blade sticking out of it. It crumpled over, straining its neck to look behind him.

"It's all about skill." Genblade smiled as he withdrew the blade, flicking it toward a nearby wall to clean the blood off of it.

He picked up Black Womb, elevating him and propping him up against the wall. He took out a small, sharp blade and jammed it into Black Womb's right side. It sliced directly through the cancerous blob that the doctor had been so concerned with, and a small -shink- sound indicated that it went clean through the wall as well. Genblade let go of the Womb, letting the blade prop him up, its flesh tugging around it.

"This was absolutely pathetic. If you're gonna keep going with power over skill, there's a couple of things you should be made aware of. Number one..."

Shunk. Genblade stabbed Black Womb in the arm. The creature's head raised, fully awake for the first time in several moments and really listening now, wanting to scream but unable to make the right sound.

"...your right side is your weak spot. It's where your true self, the real Black Womb, resides. But you probably figured that out. Number two..."

Shunk. He stabbed it through the other arm.

"...That healing factor of yours'll only go so far. If you tax it too much, or if I do, it'll simply cut out. Number three..."

Shunk. He stabbed it through both feet, pinning them to each other and the wall.

"...Nobody, I repeat, NOBODY escapes death."

Genblade stepped back and admired his work. Black Womb stood there, his body pinned into a cross position.

Black Womb's mind reeled. He couldn't focus on anything, his vision was blurry, and black around the edges. He felt the healing factor cut out. He lifted his head to face his attacker.

"A crucifixion," Genblade sneered, stroking his chin as he admired his work. "It'd almost be poetic, if it wasn't so damn funny."

A voice crackled to life over a nearby intercom, just out of sight. "Excellent work, Adam... Excellent work."

Black Womb stared down at the cold metal floor, now wishing that he could merely stand on it. It glared at its reflection in the blood, distorted and obtuse. It reflected how the creature felt, beaten both physically and psychologically.

Its blood mingled with that of the doctor's assistants, splattered all over the walls and the floor, making it look like a scene from a B-list horror movie. As it stared down at the reflection, its eyes swelled in shock. Its body began to convulse and throb. Slowly and painfully, it began to transform into Xander Drew again. The dark liquid that had been clinging to him ever since this nightmare began finally let go as if it had just lost its grip. It splashed to the floor, revealing his flesh starting with his feet and working its way up to its eyes where it disappeared.

All that was left was Xander, naked and pinned to the wall, blood hemorrhaging from his wounds.

His eyes remained black for a moment, but when it passed they returned to normal. His skin was still covered with a thin layer of blood, a film left over from the change. He gasped for air as sweat and blood rolled down his face. He screamed long and loud, as if he was feeling the crucifix for the first time. Blood began to flow liberally from his hands, feet and side. As the floor around him began to fill with it, he noticed a small drain under him which it was all flowing into. His body began to shake as it ran out of fluids, his eyes rolling into the back of his head.

Genblade stepped into the Womb's field of vision again, bending down and placing his hand flat into the puddle of tar-like blood. When he brought it around to look at it, it was covered completely in the shiny black liquid, and he found himself staring at it intently.

"That should be enough, Adam. I believe it time to begin phase two," came the voice behind the intercom.

Genblade stepped out of the darkness, a corrupt smile on his face.

†⟨†

"Engen.com. Huh."

"What is it?" Mike demanded. They had been waiting for a background check on the web site for several hours, and the exhaustion had long since started to fray at him. It was all he could do not to think about the events of the previous night. "What have you found?"

"Nothing," Tim answered, turning his screen a little. "It's just someone's home page. Aside from the animation, it's a poorly done home page. There's nothing unusual here."

Mike sighed, then turned the computer screen so that he could see. The Engen symbol danced around the window to the tune of *Minority* by Green Day. He examined it carefully, and after a second, he noticed something in the corner. "What's that?"

"What?" Cathy and Tim said simultaneously, each shifting a little in their seats.

"That spider symbol in the corner," he said, even as he clicked on it. Automatically, a single message came up onto the screen: Black Womb Lives.

"That's it? That's what you have to tell me?" Tim growled, as much at the web site as at Mike.

"Black Womb. That was written on the wall where Jamie..." Mike stopped, looking at the floor. "Where the first murder took place."

Tim frowned reluctantly. "There could be something, I guess. But it doesn't give us any leads."

Cathy sighed, turning his laptop toward her so that she could finally get a look, mouthing the words 'Black Womb lives' to herself over and over again.

"We've got nothing," Mike agreed, clenching his fist and almost punching the wall, stopping himself right before he did so.

"Like I said," Tim agreed, motioning in his direction.

Cathy frowned. "You said... the Jacobies adopted kids... right?"

"Yes," Tim answered, rubbing the bridge of his nose while he mentally calculated the hours he had gone without sleep.

She clicked her tongue against the roof of her mouth. "Then... is there any way to find out where these kids are now? Or where they were adopted from?"

Mike and Tim exchanged a look.

Tim leaned forward and opened up a web browser, typing in his user ID quickly. After only a moment of looking, he responded to her query. "I can't find out who they adopted... there's just no record... but they were all adopted from the same place. A little convent upstate."

"That's where Xander was adopted from," Mike said, leaning in and squinting at the screen. "And me."

Cathy rolled that around in her head for a minute. "Who are Xander's birth parents?"

Again, Tim typed for a moment. "No record."

"How does that happen? Is it just, like, a drop the baby on the doorstep kinda deal?"

Tim's eyes went large as he realized what she was getting at. "Yes. It would be something just like that, actually."

"So... what's to stop us from going to that place and just looking for a big building with Engen stamped across it?" Mike said, giving a nod to his girl.

Tim paused, taking a long look at each of them, trying to gauge how serious they actually were. He got up and grabbed his coat.

⋏⋌

"Interesting. Most interesting indeed," the man on the intercom said, as he observed Xander getting shocked by the electrified bars of his cell. He brought an oxygen mask to his face and sucked back air, steadying his voice before he pressed the intercom's 'On' switch so that Xander could hear him.

"Welcome home, Subject 08276," he said in an overly dramatic voice. "You probably don't remember, but this cell was once the home of you and your dear mother."

"My mother?" Xander gasped, smoke rising up from his back.

There was a slight pause on the intercom. Suddenly, the rough voice returned. "Welcome home, 08276. Welcome home, Black Womb."

The intercom switched off, leaving Xander with more questions than answers. He rose up and looked down at himself, taking note of several red stains on the paper gown he was clothed in. He looked around his cell. It was exceedingly simplistic in its nature, with three concrete walls that obviously held wiring for the electrical steel bars that covered his exit. The floor and ceiling were both metal. The room itself was only about five meters cubed, with no furniture or plumbing.

He stared at the bars.

He stared at them until they went from being solid lines dissecting his vision to watery, unfocussed slashes. There was an ache building in the centre of his chest the more he looked at them. They filled him with an anxiety that dispelled all rational thought, until for a moment all he could think was: the *bars*.

He sniffed back hard and forced his eyes to refocus. Slowly, thought returned to him.

But the anxiety remained, no matter how much he tried to bury it.

Electrified bars needed to be hollow to have wiring inside of them and to better conduct electricity, he recalled. So the only real problem was getting past the electricity. Xander frowned.

"Genius, man. Genius," he mumbled to himself.

Still, he searched his brain for something, *anything* he could use. Finding nothing, he walked over to the bars. Touching one lightly with his index finger, he pulled it away immediately as the electricity coursed through his fingertips. He touched another bar with the same result, then pulled back and stroked his chin.

He poked at the bar at the top, near the ceiling. There was still a shock, but it wasn't as potent. If there was a place to short it out, it'd be there. There was still the problem of what to do with this knowledge. He sat down on the metal floor.

"Ow!" he yelped, jumping to his feet. Something had poked at him. He examined the floor and found nothing, then reached around to his back and smiled.

Safety pins.

He pulled the top one out of the back of his gown. The top of it opened and he glanced down at his chest. To his relief, many of the wounds were healing. Except the ones from the crucifixion.

He stepped up to the bars and inserted the pin to the top. He pulled away automatically with shock, but the electricity held the pin there. As he watched the pin began to glow white hot, until finally the bar's generator exploded in an array of white and blue sparks from which he had to shield his eyes momentarily.

He stepped up to the bars again and attempted to stretch them. To his surprise, they slid open. He stepped out and looked around.

There was no one in either corridor, in any direction. Both sides seemed equally long and equally intimidating, stretching on forever. So he just went with his gut and chose right. He started to run but his body rebelled, smashing him to the floor. He looked down at his feet, which were now bleeding again from the crucifixion wounds.

"Dammit. Where's my guardian monster when I need him?" he uttered in self-pity as he began to crawl along the floor. Inwardly, he thought, *It hurts. It hurts so bad. But I can't stop. Just like Sara always said. You can never stop. I swear I'll kill that monster for what he did to you.*

"Just like his mother," chuckled the voice behind the intercom, before letting out a massive, hacking cough. "An admirable try, my boy. But nobody escapes from Alpha Quadrant twice in one lifetime."

He pressed a small red button on his control panel, and a buzzer began to sound throughout the facility.

Xander heard the buzzer and forced himself to his feet, despite the incredible amount of pain that it caused. He made his way to the end of the corridor already gasping for breath, then looked around for options.

Again, it was a simple choice of left or right. He thought he heard something and turned around quickly, sending shoots of pain up and down his spine. He thought that he saw something out of the corner of his eye, but he couldn't be sure. Turning back around, he decided to once again go right.

He limped to the end of that hallway, to a large yellow door. A gold plated plaque on it read: STORAGE. He opened it slowly and stepped inside.

It looked like a warehouse, but with no visible exits that he could see. Large wooden crates were stacked up almost to the ceiling and there was moving equipment everywhere. He walked to the middle of the first column.

He heard the faint sound of scuttling footsteps and turned around quickly. It was like thousands of crabs all clambering toward him at once, their tiny legs pounding against the tile. Or spiders. It could have been spiders, too.

The door that he came in through was swinging, back and forth, then came to a slow stop.

Somebody's here.

Xander turned around slowly, surveying his situation and his environment.

The crates seemed to go on for forever and ever, like a large wooden stairway. There were gaps where he could see through to the next column and when he looked out through them, all he could see was a long, slender hallway filled with more wooden crates.

He leaned on the box in front of him to get a better look. The cover rattled slightly with a clunk. He reached his nails under the lid and began to pull up. Almost instantly, pain began to shoot up his arms from his wrists. Blood poured fresh again, and he let a swear pass through his blood spattered lips. The cover finally popped off, revealing that it was filled with items that appeared to be bottles, all wrapped in a thick layer of soft gauze. Taking the prime opportunity, he unwrapped some gauze and wrapped it around his wrists. When they were done, he applied some to his heels, the cuts on which had stretched and bled with every step he'd made, and then finally to his side. The makeshift bandages almost instantly filled with blood, but they seemed to be helping.

He glanced down at what was in the jar.

It was a heart.

He jerked back with shock, dropping the jar to the floor. It shattered with an ear splitting sound that echoed throughout the entire facility. Formaldehyde splattered onto his cuts, causing a slight burning sensation as he backed into the row of crates behind him.

He felt a sudden rush of wind and turned around, but there was nobody there. He felt cold. He began to turn around and thought he saw something in the next row out of the corner of his eye and followed it. Again, nothing. He ran to the end of the column, turned the corner, and gazed down the next row. Nothing. He looked down the next. Again nothing. He kept running down the same direction, trying to trap his follower. It occurred to him that given his condition that this may not have been the wisest tactic, but he had to know.

The columns ended abruptly.

There was nobody to be seen. Then it dawned upon him: he could have easily doubled back... and followed him. He stopped dead in his tracks and slowly began to turn around. He closed his eyes, expecting that when he opened them, Genblade would be raining down hell on him. He fully believed that it would be the last thing he would ever see. Coming to a halt, he slowly opened his eyes.

Nothing.

Nothing but the bare hallway. He let out a sigh of relief.

-clunk, clunk-

The sound came from above.

Xander looked up just in time to see the crate fall.

"Get up," said the soft, soothing, feminine voice.

The voice triggered a memory deep within him. He had gotten into a fight with Grendel when he was twelve years old. He had given Grendel a black eye, but with one punch, Grendel had given him a broken nose. He had hit the ground hard and closed his eyes. The voice had come to his ears like a sweet melody that man could never hear, because no music made after would ever compare. There was a slight giggle in Sara's voice as she said the words.

"Get up."

A voice like springtime. The warm, soft... just good feeling that came with springtime. Like the sun's rays on your face.

He opened his eyes and through his blurred, painful vision, he thought he saw her standing over him with that cute smile on her face. He smiled as the voice came again, but this time there was an edge on it. He felt a sharp pain in his leg, finally opening his eyes all the way.

An athletic woman loomed over him. She was Asian, with almond eyes and a perfect, thinly honed muscular body. She had a long ponytail which swerved down and wrapped around her body. She was dressed much like Genblade was, in skintight leather, only hers was dark red with black edges.

The handles of twin katana blades protruded from holsters on her back, the straps crossing her chest with an x. She removed one of the blades and pointed it at him. It had four gold spikes coming off of the handle making the legs of a spider, with two rubies making up the body and head. "I said, get up."

He slowly rose to his feet to face her. "Mrs. Genblade, I presume."

She struck him hard and fast with the broad side of her blade.

"You may call me Spider," she said coldly. That voice

was so smooth, so beautiful... it almost didn't matter. As he crumpled to the floor, she looked down at him. "What could he possibly see in the likes of you, you impotent cur?"

"What?" he stammered.

"Nothing," she smiled. She would have had a beautiful smile, if not for her eyes, which betrayed her sinister intent. "The weapon in your blood has been depleted as a result of your inexperience and carelessness. When it has healed your rather extensive wounds, it will return to you. It has not yet, which makes this a drastically unfair fight."

She unsheathed her second blade and held it out.

He stared at it for a moment, then took it from her.

She backed up from him a few feet then stood still, glaring at him. He gripped the sword in his hands, attempted to swirl it around like on TV, and dropped it immediately.

She chuckled at the foolish attempt, watching him with fascinated amusement.

He picked it up again and held it straight. His chest rising with a deep breath, he lunged at her with a force that surprised even him, striking at her with the blade.

She lifted her own to block it, creating a sudden spark as metal met metal.

"Good," she said curtly, as if she were teaching him.

They both pushed away and she jumped at him, making one clean and graceful swipe with the sword.

He tried to lift his to defend himself, but he wasn't fast enough and her blade cut at his elbow. He felt it scrape against the bone and cringed in a sudden rush of pain and adrenaline. He swung back, but she curved her body and jumped away casually. He lunged at her a second time. Again, she blocked him with her sword.

"Better," she said again, suppressing a laugh.

They pressed against each other, neither willing to give up, until she kicked him in the side and sent him into a pile of crates. The wood splintered beneath the force of his weight and he let a deep groan from his throat. Formaldehyde leaked from broken bottles inside the crate as she dashed up to him, placing the razor sharp edge of her blade against his throat.

He glared at her, hatred in his eyes. She leaned her head in and kissed him lightly, then flipped backward, landing in a fighting stance.

He hurled himself at her, slashing with his sword.

She jumped over it.

He lashed out again.

She ducked under it.

Finally, she slashed back. He pulled away, but her blade still nicked the gauze bandages. They fell to the ground, their blood slathered surface splashing the concrete floor. He looked at the palm of his hand, wiggling his fingers. No blood. Not even a scar. His wrist was healed.

He sneered, then turned back toward her. "I think it's time you saw what I'm *really* made of."

He clenched his fists until the thin pads of his fingers dug into his palms. His heart began to pump so hard that he could feel it in his ears, drowning out the mechanical cackle of the madwoman across from him. His eyes pulsed with it as his breath became shallow and his veins became tight. He could feel them all, the pressure building all over his body until he felt like he was about to burst.

Nothing happened.

"Ngh," he grunted painfully, he cheeks flushed and red as his pulse began to slow again.

"What's the matter, little boy? Can't summon the demon in your blood?" Spider laughed. She thrust herself at him again.

Then he realized just what she had said. The demon in his blood... *I've got it.*

He raised his blade up to eye level and ran his wrist along it.

Spider stopped in her tracks, watching him with wide eyed interest.

As the sword slit the vein, blood poured down his arm. At first it was red, then it was suddenly blackened. His face cringed in pain as his pupils grew to envelope his entire eye. The blackness seeped from his arm to the rest of his body and then to his head. Three red slits appeared to slice through his face, each glowing. They opened to form glowering eyes and a mouth. Long, sharp teeth grew in from the top and bottom of the gaping gums.

"Black Womb lives."

Spider looked onward at the Black Womb in awe. She smiled, licking her lips. "Now I think I see what he sees in you."

She jumped at him. This time, he was the one to jump over her swing.

Her face twisted angrily as he jumped so high that he landed on a stack of crates. Doing a flip off of them, he propelled himself toward Spider and kicked her in the face.

She sprawled backward, slipped on the formaldehyde that had spilled on the floor, then turned and looked at him with hatred burning in her slanted eyes.

He was crouching across the hall, staring at her. He slowly reached over and grabbed a large chunk of wood from the shattered crate.

As Spider got up, he tackled her, sending them both flying through wood and glass. He raised the wooden stake high above his head, prepared to bring it down onto Spider. She caught it between her hands an inch in front of her face. Pushing the wood backward abruptly, she smacked Black Womb in the face with it. He took a step backward, then regained himself. He looked at her, her face a mess of small cuts and her ponytail now ragged. She wiped a spot of blood from the side of her face, then smeared it onto her blade.

She got up and swiftly threw the blade at Black Womb, who tried to jump out of the way, but was too slow.

The blade sliced through the corner of his side and his face distorted from pain. Claws protruded from each fingertip and he started whipping at the air around Spider wildly with them. She jumped high into the air, coming down onto his shoulders. He got up and turned to her, then picked up her sword and prepared to lunge at her when a burst of blue electricity ripped through his spinal column. He slammed to the floor and Genblade loomed over him, continuously stinging at him with his taser.

"That's enough playing around, Spider. The master requests an audience with our dear old friend, 08276 here."

They both laughed. Spider walked up to Genblade, kissing him passionately on the lips. She put her arms around him, then quickly snatched the taser away.

"But I want to play," she said with a pouting child's voice. She dug the taser into Xander's back and turned it on. His eyes lit up with blue.

Her smile widened.

"Okay," Tim sighed, shuffling through a pile of papers. "We have about five hundred references to something called the Black Womb in all of these files, but the first two hundred and fifty contradict the last two hundred and fifty."

He buried his head in his arms and tossed his glasses onto the table in front of him.

"Alright, but there is one continued reference," Cathy noted, staring down at her own stack of papers.

"There is?" Mike said, leaning over her shoulder, giving her a little kiss on the cheek.

"What?" Tim asked, getting up from his chair.

"A date," she said thoughtfully. "March 7th... fifteen years ago."

They all looked puzzled for a moment.

"Hey," Mike said, his eyes brightening. "That'd be around the time Xander was born."

"Quick," Tim said, walking over to her. "What document was that from?"

"Um... something called Alpha Quadrant up near the Canadian border," she replied.

"And about six miles from where the orphanage was," Mike murmured, stroking his top lip with his index finger.

"Alright then," Tim smirked, heading for the door.

Floating. He felt like he was floating. That was the first thing that Xander thought when he woke up. Every inch of his body ached. He tried to move, but pain shot up and down his spine, making him wish that he were dead. He struggled to open his eyes and when he did the light shone at him, bright and burning.

"Hi, lover," came Spider's voice, her evil cackle echoing through the stone walls.

The light was lowered and he could see Spider and Genblade looming over him, smiling. There was someone else too...

"AAAARRRGHH!" he shouted, as pain shot through his body.

"A reminder," Genblade said coldly. "Don't try and escape. Those electrical currents will eventually kill you." His teeth showed as his smile grew. They were pointed, each one sharpened to a razor's edge.

Xander's body went limp. He was covered in a thin layer of blood again, his head splitting from repeated blows. He could feel blood pumping out of his ears and down the side of his neck.

Spider reached out and took some of it onto her finger.

"Fear is so much more interesting an emotion than hope, isn't it, Adam?" she said as she put the bloodied finger into her mouth. "Tastier too."

Xander felt like throwing up. The mixture of a blood filled stomach and what she had just done causing him to have to fight back the urging of his gut.

"You look just like your mother, my child," came a voice from the darkness. It was the exact same voice that had come over the intercom before. Thick, raspy, and nearly hushed to the point of a whisper. "She fought us too, you know. But from her, we learned. Taking people from the outside leaves them with a sense of resistance. They long for the relationships, friends and lovers that the outside world brings. After your mother's death, we decided to scrap all those projects and start anew."

Xander squinted his eyes, trying to penetrate the darkness. "Who are you?"

He laughed, then let out a wracking cough. It chilled Xander to the bone. "Soon son, soon. Now, as I was saying, we learned a lot from your mother's escape. When we won the gene war, there were a few section heads that were nervous about the damage that would be done if word got out about project Black Womb. About you. It had almost happened once before in the seventies and almost led to the collapse of our entire research and development department. They were idiots, all of them. Old fogies set to their mindless ways and then bold enough to call their work a new genesis. They had to go. How else could one rise above in this world, after all? Soon I was a section head myself and one of the controlling stockholders at Engen Industries."

"Engen?" Xander murmured, the words striking a chord.

"Also known as Alpha Quadrant. You see, I believed that you and the others on the outside could be assimilated into life on the inside. But first, we had to sever all of your links to the outside. We had to end your relationships with those you love, those you hate... everyone associated with you. This would leave you susceptible to the mind tempering needed for the final step of assimilation."

Xander looked over at Genblade. "So you sent this walking militia to kill off my friends."

"No, boy. We needed to do research. I found you on-line after months of searching through chat sites. Finally I found you and, using a user name that was not easily traceable, I approached you and eventually gained your trust."

"Soul," Xander said, cursing inwardly.

"Precisely. Then, my dear Spider began contacting your friends via the internet, making them trust you even less."

"Spider."

"Exactly. Thinking we would never meet, you felt free to talk to me about your friends, your loved ones, and even people you didn't like much at all. We thought it wise to begin there, sending Spider to herd the cattle to a certain spot for Genblade to mow them down."

"Jamie," Xander whispered as shock ran down through his face.

"You hated him because Sara loved him. Pathetic, teenage drivel! You were bred to be better than that! Cur! But what else could I expect from you, really? Whether you blame it on nature or nurture, you didn't really have a chance. You were made of junk DNA and raised by white trash... How could we hope for you to grow into anything but garbage?"

The thoughts crashed upon him like a wave onto the shore. It was his fault. All of this. Jamie's death, Carl

Dent's death, the attacks on Mike, Cathy, Sud, Tommy... all his fault. And Sara. At the thought of her, he wanted to cry. He'd killed her. He may not have actually done the deed, but he may as well have pulled the trigger. It was his fault that she was dead. Dead.

"You fucker. You killed all these people... just to get to me?" The hatred burned in his eyes.

"No," Genblade said, his smile growing ferociously as he wrapped his hands around Spider, letting them trickle up and down her front. "I killed Jamie Dawkins. I loved it. He came apart so easily I could taste it. That old couple and your little whore, yeah I did them too. But that was it."

"Then who?!?" Xander shouted, pulling against his restraints. Electricity surged up from them, forcing him back down. "Who did it? Give me a name. I'll kill him right after I'm done with you, you sick son of a..."

"You want a name?" Genblade interrupted, laughing hysterically. "You want the name?"

"Just give me the damn name!" he shouted. This time when the electricity surged, he ignored it. The emotional pain outweighed the physical.

"Xander Drew."

CHAPTER NINE
TRUTH

All was quiet. The words sunk deep.

"What?" Xander spat, his upper lip curling.

"It was you. Or rather, the 'savior' within your veins."

"You're a liar. And a killer. Give me one good reason why *I* should believe *you*."

"Because," came the voice from the darkness. "It's true. The Black Womb's consciousness resides within you. You have remarkable skills, my boy, but not even you can control a Black Womb twenty-four hours a day. These past few months ever since you hit puberty, when you sleep and your mind is overpowered by that of the Black Womb, he escapes. It's easy to identify. When you call him, that is, when you have his body surrounding yours but you still remain in control, your eyes have a reddish tint to them. But Black Womb's consciousness is let out when you stop thinking rationally, when you get extremely emotional or when you sleep. On one of his outings, the Womb happened upon Genblade murdering Jamie Dawkins. Spider and Genblade thought it to be an extraordinary bit of luck and allowed you to watch and participate as they stripped him of his usable organs. The Black Womb's savage instincts took over. He had gotten a taste of the blood that he was meant to *bathe* in and he wanted more. There were other programming methods, of course. Engen.com filled the Womb portion of your consciousness with subliminal messages while that screen was flashing. But in the end, it was that simple act of getting blood on your hands that brought out the real you. So each time you slept, he went out to claim another. Or at least to try. It seems that your consciousness had some residual effects on Black Womb. When it came time to strike down someone you loved, Mike Harris, he could not. A pity."

"M-me?" Xander stammered, the words cutting into him worse than any of Genblade's daggers ever could. He had maimed and killed all those people. Not indirectly, but in pure form. "Kill me."

"Oh! No my boy, no," the figure laughed. "Not quite yet." Then, his captor's voice became surprisingly sympathetic. "I wanted to die once, too. Once, when I was just a security guard, waiting for death to claim me as I lay in that hospital bed..." then his voice perked up. "But you must remember, my boy. It wasn't you. It was that bloody bastard in your veins that did it. That's why I brought you here."

"What?" Xander balked, again searching the darkness. "What are you talking about?"

"I think my predecessors did a bad thing. We let you go. Out there, in countless orphanages, you didn't get the training that you needed to harness the Black Womb. You didn't know what was happening inside of your body every minute of every day. But alas, this can be remedied. You can be rid of it."

"Not sure I follow."

"If you willingly give up the Black Womb and someone else, at the same time, willingly takes it, I can surgically remove it from you. I can relieve you of your curse."

"How?"

"In the years since that lowly security guard Abner Jacobs was injured, I have become a man of science. With the help of Engen scientists, I mastered the darkness. Even found a way to purify it and all other diseases from unborn children, thus producing my genetic Adam and Eve."

"Genblade and Spider." Xander's eyes widened as he looked over at the two assassins as they kissed.

"But they were incomplete, missing organs. It created artificial ones for their use, but they were still inferior."

"So you strip mined your victims... and mine... to put their organs into these two?" He had to strain the word 'mine' out of his lips.

"Yes. My goal is to have them reproduce. To create a new, perfect society, under a new god. Me."

"You're sick."

He laughed. "You don't know the half of it," he coughed. It was sick, like he was throwing up a lung.

"Something wrong?"

Electricity jolted through the shackles. "Quiet. Anyway, I finally got the last thing I needed for my children. Or, more appropriately, for their children. Ovaries."

"Sara."

Spider smiled at him. "Mmm. I can feel how much she

wanted you to touch them, Xander. To taste them."

Xander lowered his head, forcing his eyes not to well up with tears.

"Yes. You should be proud. Your friend will live on in Spider's children."

He processed this. "But, I don't understand. There were way more organs than you needed. And what do you need Black Womb for?"

"Will you give the creature up?"

Xander thought about it. Hadn't he done enough harm? Like the guy said, he couldn't control this thing. He couldn't even restrain it. This guy, whoever he was, he had already melded it into life. "Okay."

Genblade walked over and cut Xander across the stomach.

Xander's back arched and he screamed in pain. Blood flowed from the wound which had already been opened too many times this night. The blood ran down his legs, mixing with the red film the Black Womb had left behind.

Then, finally, the man came out of the darkness.

He was in pieces, no part of his form whole. His head was only half there, a line having been ripped down his nose and dug out as if somebody had taken a shovel to the left side of his head. His mouth didn't end, it just melted into the mauled flesh that was his face. There were gaping holes of ripped flesh covering his bald head, giving way to his skull. Blood poured freely from those holes. There was a hunch on his back so huge it rose slightly above his hairline. It had stretched the flesh to the near breaking point and was covered in hideous warts and boils. His ridiculously muscular arms were covered in places where skin just melted away, showing his actual muscles as they rippled. His stomach and rib cage were missing, revealing the convulsing organs within. His heart pumped so fast that there was hardly a space between beats. His legs were much the same as his arms. They were covered in torn laboratory pants, the tears revealing exposed tendons and blisters. He looked like a cross between an Ogre and a corpse.

"Christ. What are you?" Xander asked, astonished.

"Call me Alpha. You see, I needed all those extra organs for myself," he said as he inserted the Womb organ into his lower chest, easy considering it wasn't covered. "You see, I was a guard on duty the day your bitch of a mother saw fit to leave us. She also left us a parting gift. She blew our power generator, killing all of your brothers and sisters that were in stasis. She prevented Engen from ever creating a soldier capable of bringing you back. She truly loved you."

For the first time, Alpha's words felt good. He had always assumed that his mother had abandoned her child out of hatred and bitterness, not circumstance.

"But I was on duty in that sector. She literally blew half of me away. The preservatives in the goop that kept your siblings in stasis kept me alive long enough for Engen scientists to find me and rebuild me. One took me under his wing and taught me everything he knew. He became like a father to me as I became a son to him. By the time my condition was stable, I knew everything I needed to do to rise to the top of the company and get my vengeance on your mother... by killing you."

Black Womb

"I still don't get what you need Black Womb for."

"I'm falling apart," he said, gesturing toward himself. "The Womb's healing capabilities, which I saw fit to test in your battles with Genblade and Spider (hence the crucifixion), will heal me. It will meld all of my stolen body parts into one ... my own."

Even as he spoke, Alpha's face began to flow like liquid, reforming itself into a normal one. A thin covering of skin formed over his exposed stomach, then getting thicker and thicker. His muscles covered over with flesh as blood flowed from his mouth and ears. Black blood. The substance oozed over him as he laughed, deep and hysterical. When he was covered, a large jaw formed that, when opened, stretched down to his chest and displayed a full ten rows of jagged, yellow teeth. His eyes were gigantic and red, meaning that he was in complete control. "Alpha lives."

It was all Xander could do to keep from urinating in his pants. His gut was slowly closing itself as a final gift from the now absent Black Womb. His clothes were splattered in blood and vomit. His eyes were filled with tears, but more than that, they were full of hatred.

"Now you understand, boy. The cycle is complete. And I can finally offer an end to your suffering." He snapped his fingers. "Spider, do with him as you will. Genblade, you're with me."

Genblade paused, clenching a fist and stepping closer to Xander, before finally turning and obeying his master.

Spider stood over him, smiling.

Xander was fully content with letting her kill him. He had done enough damage. It was time to let him rot in hell, in peace. He lay on the floor and stared upward at Spider. He closed his eyes as she drew her sword and waited for sweet, sweet oblivion... until he heard that harsh, rough voice cut through his ears.

"You know," Genblade said as he walked toward the door. "You can't start a new, more powerful civilization without wiping out the old one. Out with the old, in with the new, and all that crap."

Alpha snapped his fingers, and Genblade followed him out the doorway.

Xander stared at the door for a moment, then let his head fall again. He clicked his burned, bleeding tongue against the roof of his mouth as Genblade's words sunk in, ignoring the pain it caused.

"So that Spider and Genblade can produce a new era in humanity, they'll have to obliterate this era," Xander whispered to himself.

There were still so many people alive that he cared about. Mike, Cathy, his Mother and Father, Derek.... They would all be wiped out. Along with everyone else on earth.

"And I just gave Alpha the power to do it."

Spider swung her sword down.

Xander felt something twitch within his brain. That tiny spark he'd kept hidden from the world from long before Alpha entered his life, the part of him that kept him after Sara and telling himself that tomorrow would be better. Even though Sara was gone and tomorrow would never be better than yesterday, that part of him was still alive. He clapped his hands together and caught the blade with his palms. "Sorry lady, but no more blood goes on my hands tonight."

He flipped up onto his feet and turned to face Spider, pointing her sword at her. She reached behind her and pulled out her second blade, then lunged forward, slicing at the air around him.

He looked down and saw she had cut the fabric of his shirt above his heart. He allowed himself a small sigh of relief, then swung back in retaliation.

She did a back flip to avoid the hit, landing on her hands. She pushed off with her palms, doing another flip and landing on her feet again, making the whole thing look effortless. Xander stood his ground.

He remembered all of the times he had fought Mike in Marble Mutant Super Heroes. He'd pick Obsidian (because he's *Obsidian*, of course) and Mike' d always pick Stone Spider. Obsidian had the claws and all of these cool moves like 'dark rage' and 'abyss x'... but he'd never get a chance to use them. As soon as he got anywhere near Mike's Stone Spider, he'd start to cream him using 'ultimate spider', where Stone Spider just whipped around the screen, hitting Obsidian hundreds of times as he went. Stone Spider's strength always relied on the fact that he was so fast and so agile, that anytime you got anywhere near him, he'd have you. Just like Spider. If he went near her in this weakened state, she'd slice him up like a sausage. He'd have to use a tactic he learned while fighting Mike: *wait for the opponent to come to you.*

He stared at her and she stared back, both of their swords ready to draw first blood.

She jumped at him again, but this time he was ready. He lifted his arms and let her pass by him. Her sword nicked his side and he cringed. It was so much more pain-ful now, with the knowledge that without Black Womb, that one slice could be lethal. He turned around and stabbed at her. His sword punched through the skin of her thigh.

"Ahh!" she cried, buckling a little to one side. "You can't do this. You are an impotent dog waiting to be put down."

He hopped backward, widening the space between them. "In case nobody ever told you, Spider... every dog has his day."

She glared at him, applying pressure to her wound for a moment. There was hatred in her eyes as she realized he had gotten the better of her. She stood straight, raised her sword, and in one swift motion she threw it at his head.

It missed, zooming past his ear and digging itself into the pavement. He turned to watch it go and when he turned back, she was almost on top of him. He quickly raised his sword to deflect her attack, but it was too late.

Her fist smacked hard against the side of his face, causing the skin to split.

He fell to the pavement, skinning his joints. As the flesh pulled away from his knees, he ground his teeth so hard that a chunk of his left molar snapped off and bounced down his throat.

She picked up his sword and lunged at him with it. He rolled to the side, her blade slicing into the pavement. When she tried again, he rolled back to where he had started. He looked up at her as she raised her blade high above her head. He kicked out with both legs, smacking into both her kneecaps. She fell forward slightly and he ran to the wall and scooped at her sword handle, trying desperately to pull it from the concrete. He braced himself against the wall with one foot and he yanked on the sword violently, struggling against the stone that held onto it. He glanced over his shoulder and saw that she was rapidly recovering, even trying to stand. The wall finally gave and the sword slid into his hands. He gripped it firmly and turned to face her. Their swords itched for the other's flesh. He lowered his to the ground, until the very tip scraped against the blood-smeared concrete.

-tink!-

-tink-. Against the pavement. Xander smiled as Spider's eyes grew wide. She kept her focus on him, using all the training her mind had ever absorbed.

-tink-. -tink-. -tink-. -tink-.

Her eyebrow started to twitch as the instinct to look down began to overwhelm her. She calmed herself, breathing deeply. -tink-. Slow, rhythmic breath. -tink-. Her eye twitched to the side, only for a moment.

Xander smirked, enjoying the use of his enemy's tactics against them.

Finally she gave in to temptation and looked at the source of the sound.

When she looked back at Xander, he was gone.

She stared out into the darkness surrounding her. Slowly, the hatred in her eyes faded away to something else: fear. She began slashing at the darkness wildly, screaming as she did so. She stopped in the centre of the room, the light shimmering down her long hair. She stared wide-eyed into the darkness.

She twirled around, then back again - always convinced that he was behind her. Sweat dotted her brow and traveled down in itchy trails as she fought to keep it out of her eyes, scanning the darkness wildly for any motion.

"Where are you!?" she bellowed into the black, panic coming over her. As powerful as she was, she looked small and fragile now, the way a tree looks massive but a single leaf like nothing at all.

Light bathed the room for a quick moment and she thought she heard a door close.

She spun around to face it, her blade in front of her.

The window in the door stared at her like one great luminescent eye pinning her in place. Her breath was still tight in her chest and her hair clung to her face, which was now drenched in a fresh smattering of panic sweat. She didn't know where it had come from, but she could feel the chill of it on her skin and the salt of it on her lips.

She tried to hold the blade in front of her steady, but it wavered as adrenaline shook her nerves until her arm quivered. The blade wavered back and forth like a tuning fork.

And there was quiet.

She let out a slow sigh of relief and lowered the sword.

"Fuck," she cursed, then stormed toward the door after him.

-click-

She turned around and bumped right into Xander.

He plunged the sword into her. She let out a small, almost inaudible yelp.

Her head fell forward onto the nape of his neck, and he could see the sword protrude from her back.

Her mouth and eyes opened wide in a look of pure shock. He removed the sword and laid her carefully onto the pavement floor. Blood gushed from her open wound and she stared up at her killer. Her mouth opened as if she was about to say something, then closed, her lip gloss shining in the intense light. Her eyes gazed upward, then they rolled into her head.

Xander stepped into the darkness. Finding the door, he exited the room, sliding his sword along the floor as he went.

ʎ‹›ʎ

In another part of the building, Genblade and Alpha walked toward their destination. Suddenly, alarms began blaring from everywhere.

Alpha looked downward, as if briefly mourning. "You know what this means."

Genblade's eyes filled with disappointment. "That the Black Womb has bested Spider."

Alpha slammed him against the stone wall, pressing his arm against his neck. "Never! Never call him that AGAIN! I am the Black Womb now! Do you hear me?"

"Yes, Master," Genblade said quickly, avoiding angering his creator anymore. He did a small bow as Alpha let him go. "I am sorry, Master. It will not happen again."

"Go, Genblade. Stop 08276 from ruining my plans. Do whatever it takes."

"Yes, Master," Genblade replied, pulling at his shirt.

He turned and jogged back down the corridor the way they had come.

Alpha turned to face a door marked REACTOR and walked in.

Alarms ringing in his ears and electric surges shooting up his side from where Spider had cut him, Xander ran up the halls in a constant state of pain and confusion, not even knowing if he was headed in the right direction. He came to a four-way intersection and tripped, despite all his attempts to keep his steady pace. He fell to his knees. Pain shot through them as the spots where he had skinned them became irritated again. He clenched his teeth to fight back a yelp and suddenly, the alarms just... stopped. He stood up and turned slowly, looking in each of the three directions and back the way he came.

Out of the corner of his left eye, he thought he saw something.

When he looked down that hallway, it was gone. Something ran past the hallway in front of him. He felt the breeze of speed as the person passed by. A cackle of insane laughter echoed through the hallways, making it impossible to tell which direction it came from.

"Genblade," Xander said under his breath. He raised his sword to eye-level, prepared for the oncoming battle. Beads of sweat began to form on his scalp as his eyes darted from hallway to hallway, trying to catch a glimpse of his predator. Then he remembered the words Cathy once used for predators:

'They're just people, like you or me. I have this dream, where I'm supposed to be some kind of protector. But I always fail to protect the prey from the predator. I think it had something to do with a past life.' She giggled. 'Not that I believe in that. So, anyway, the only way you could ever rise above the predator is to

become the predator. Learn to think as he thinks and you'll know his move ten moves before he makes it. Just like in chess. Not that you'd know anything about chess, the way you and Mike are always wrapped up in that bloody video game. I swear by all that's holy, someday I'll take a baseball bat to that machine-'

And the answer came to him. It was cliché, but: it takes one to know one. He had to become that which he hated most: Genblade. And to his own surprise, he actually found himself thinking, *if I were a savage, disgusting, born and bred killer, where would I be?* The answer dawned upon him like the sun dawns upon the earth each morning. *I'd be behind me.*

Xander jabbed his sword under his arm without even looking. His eyes bulged with delight as it connected, producing that same subtle tug that Spider's flesh had.

He retracted it and turned around to face Genblade. "You killed the woman I loved."

Genblade glared down at him, removing his double blade from its straps. "And you killed the woman I loved."

They circled each other for a moment. The tension hung in the air as each combatant weighed what the other had said. Xander shuddered at the thought that he and Genblade might as well have been opposite sides of the same coin. He raised his sword, which was now tarnished with the blood of both Spider and Genblade. The new Adam and Eve. Sweat bubbled from each opponent, each waiting for the other to make a move. Finally, Genblade struck. He lashed out at Xander, cutting him across the chest. The sword dug deep, clawing at the bone. Within seconds, blood had soaked through the entire chest of his shirt. Shoots of pain ran up and down Xander every few seconds, but it wasn't constant, making it impossible to tune out.

He turned to retaliate, but found that he was already on top of him. Genblade's blade came across Xander's jaw like quicksilver, slicing at the mouth and causing him to bleed violently. It hurt to breathe. All the while he struggled to remember the words that Cathy had said. *To beat him, I have to become him.* Genblade put his arm around Xander's neck, embracing him in a headlock. He drew back his sword, preparing to plunge it through his trunk. *To beat him, you must become him.* Was he a killer like Genblade? He'd killed, now not only as Black Womb, but also as Xander Drew. Did that make him any better? Or worse?

No! his mind screamed. Twisting in Genblade's grip, he brought his knee to his side. Genblade doubled over, winded from the unexpected attack. Xander drew back his own sword and in one swift motion he sliced him across the shoulder. Genblade pulled back his own sword, then dropped it from pain. The shoulder wound would not allow him to lift his own weapon in defense. Xander sliced him across the chest, making a deep incision. Blood ran freely from the wound. Xander was about to make a shot to the jaw when Genblade tackled him, using what was obviously his last iota of energy. They both flew into the concrete wall and Xander bumped his head on it. He could hear his skull crack under the pressure as Genblade lay into him with a series of stabs with his dagger. He punched three holes into Xander's torso before Xander finally kicked him off, sending him flying into the other wall.

Genblade was unconscious. *Helpless.*

Xander picked up his sword and pressed it against his enemy's neck.

"You killed the woman I love. But I did the same to you. Does that make me the same as you, Genblade?" He paused for a second, twirling his blade. For a brief moment, he thought he saw Sara reaching out to him.

"No," he said, throwing the sword aside. "Nothing can bring Sara back. There's been enough blood spilled this day."

Then he gazed up the corridor that Genblade had come from.

"Almost."

⋏⋎⋏

The room marked REACTOR was impossibly large and circular, like the inside of some giant dome. It was bordered by metal catwalks and stairways, some of which dropped off to nowhere or led back onto themselves, like something out of a M.C. Escher painting. In the centre of it all was a giant sphere made of metal plates of varying colours and qualities, some rusted beyond belief and others new and shimmering. One arm of the catwalk lead to it, and where they met there was a large control panel made up of gaggles of wires and turning parts. What had once been new and sophisticated was now crumbling and falling apart, patched up with stolen parts... much like the man who had done the patching. There were three car batteries wired into its side and long spirals of clear blue cable connecting one side of the terminal to the other. Dimmer switches and gearshifts had replaced buttons, and near the centre there was a CD player held tight to it with Bondo.

The centre of the sphere glowed nuclear green, so bright that it could barely be looked at.

Alpha stood in front of it and laughed quietly to himself.

"You're insane," Xander said from the doorway. "It's over. Your perfect world can't exist without your perfect mother. Give it up."

Alpha turned to face him. "It's funny that it should end this way. The same way it began nearly twenty years ago with your mother and I." Alpha raised his hand. Two long, black claws protruded from each wrist. "Interesting. It appears that the Womb's abilities vary from person to person." He lunged at Xander, claws outstretched. Xander barely managed to dodge it. "You're too late anyway," he laughed, cocking his head toward the reactor.

Xander turned and saw red numbers flashing on the control station's screen. It looked like it had been lifted from an old clock radio. They were counting down, and were fast approaching the minute mark.

"The core is set to expose itself. The Womb will allow me to survive that blast, but not you... and not anyone in that pathetic town of yours."

Alpha jumped toward Xander, propelled by powerfully elastic legs. He flew through the air, growling deep in his throat. Xander was barely able to jump out of the way. Alpha's claws tore at his flesh, causing blood to splatter onto the walls. Xander landed on a metal walkway that led to the reactor. He got up, holding his side and started a limped run for the control panel.

0:59

Alpha turned to face him and saw what he was trying to do. With one fluid motion, his body stretched so that it was in front of Xander, towering over him. He was all that stood between Xander and the timer. Alpha slashed at him again, this time ripping through his stomach. There was a gaping hole there now, he could feel it pulsing and seeping. Could feel the blood splashing down onto his legs. He drew back to punch Alpha, but he caught the attack in his palm. Alpha squeezed on Xander's fist, blood running from his knuckles. Then with one quick heave, he threw Xander back against the wall.

0:40

Blood gushed from a cut on his head as he tasted the coppery tang of it in his mouth. He spit out a tooth onto the metal floor. Beads of sweat began to roll down his face as the reactor powered up. He opened his eyes to see Alpha crouching in front of him. He opened his mouth, showing his monstrously pointed fangs. Alpha jumped at him with mouth open wide, biting down on Xander's leg. He screamed in terror as the creature's many rows of teeth acted like a chainsaw on the flesh and bone. He kicked at Alpha with his free leg and finally managed to beat him off. Alpha drew back a bit, growling.

0:20

Xander felt like giving up. Giving in to the monster before him. His guts in his arms, his blood on the ground... it was his time. He let out a final breath. Then, he thought of her. Of Sara. Of a conversation they had had once.

CHAPTER TEN
OUT

Xander lay on the ground, broken and beaten by Grendel, who was Sara's current boyfriend.

"When are you going to stop doing this?" she had asked him, using his shirt to wipe a bit of blood from his lip.

He looked up at her, smiling. "I guess when I start winning fights."

"Not that," she giggled, wiping more blood from his forehead. "This. Chasing after every boy I go out with like some... jealous father."

"Oh," Xander said, looking downward. I guess when you start going out with reasonable guys."

"What do you mean?"

"Gee, I wonder. Grendel, Derek, Sud, Tommy, Jamie, Travis, Cecil... the list goes on. Guys that are... Okay, but they don't deserve you. You deserve someone special. Someone who'll treat you right and make you feel good and... and not look at you like you're an object. You're better than you think you are, y'know. You deserve better."

She leaned in and kissed him on the cheek. That was the

nicest thing anyone ever said to me." She smiled. *"Make me a promise."*

"Anything."

"Don't ever give up."

"Huh?"

"Don't ever stop protecting me. And when I finally do find that guy you were talking about, protect someone else. The world needs a protector, Xander."

"I promise."

"Don't ever give up

"Don't ever give up

"Don't ever give up

"Don't ever give up…"

"I won't," he said aloud. As Alpha lunged at him, Xander reached into his pocket and pulled out one of Genblade's daggers. He thrust out, giving it every ounce of raw power he had left. The blade sunk deep into Alpha's right side, then ripped across to the left. As Alpha ripped at Xander's back, Xander reached his hand into Alpha and ripped it out. The pure essence of the Black Womb. That black and gray, smoldering lump of organ.

Alpha's eyes went wide for an instant, before shrinking back into small white marbles in the middle of his face.

The blackness lost its hold on him all at once and fell from of his body, splashing through the grates of the catwalk and down into the nothingness below. His toothless, cancerous mouth took a deep gasp before he went limp and fell to the floor. His stomach, muscles and skull were all exposed again. As Xander watched, each one seemed to sputter and die on their own.

Wincing, Xander pried open the edges of the wound that Alpha had slashed across his stomach and pushed the Womb organ inside. Black tendrils spat out of its porous surface and latched onto his large intestine, pulling itself into place and pouring out so much blackness that it flowed freely from the opening in Xander's side and out onto his legs.

His heartbeat doubled, then tripled, then began to beat so fast that it sound more like static in his ears than a drum. Only it wasn't his heart, at least not his human one. He could feel it pulsing and moving in his side, bending and kneading itself to spread more and more. And, as horrific as it was, it somehow it felt... *right*.

Black liquid began to pour from his mouth and nose, falling down onto his chest and building there a quart at a time until it covered his entire body.

"Black Womb lives."

0:10

He ran across the metal walkway to the timer and opened the hatch on it, revealing the mess of wires inside. He stared at it blankly for a moment.

0:09

He pointed a claw at the red wire, then shrugged it off.

0:08

Blue wire. He inched to it with his talon, then decided against it.

0:07

Green wire. *No,* he thought, *it's never the green wire.*

0:06

Frustration built and Xander could feel Black Womb

begin to take over.

Alpha leaned against the wall, a wry grin prying across his lips. "The blue wire!" he yelled, before finally succumbing to his wounds and slamming against the floor. Blood oozed from his lips.

Black Womb ripped at the slender cable with his hooked claw.

0:05

"Did it stop?" he wondered aloud.

0:04

"Why didn't it stop?"

0:03

He looked back in horror at Alpha, almost certain he could see the deranged man's grin, even in death.

0:02

Hope Alpha was right about Black Womb being able to survive this...

0:01

The radioactive rods in front of Xander exposed themselves, their eerie green glow filling the room. He felt his flesh start to burn as the liquid surrounding his brain boiled within his skull and his teeth rattled, trying to shake themselves free of his gums. He closed his eyes as they started to bubble and crack.

Behind him Alpha's body exploded, erupting in blue flame, then green, until eventually there was nothing left to the madman.

Here goes nothing, he thought to himself, as he felt even the Womb-skin begin to peel back, revealing the tender, weak form of Xander Drew underneath. Reaching out with both hands, he pressed down on the reactor rod.

All around him, the walls were cracking, steel and wood falling down around him as the building's foundation became weaker and weaker, getting ready to implode upon itself.

祥

Outside, police cars were surrounding the building. Suddenly, it began to fall into itself, its centre crumbling away one piece at a time. There was a roar like thunder and a single wave of intense heat as the chunks of falling metal and plaster got larger and larger, crashing onto the floor inside. Long cracks started to spread their way up from the foundation, jumping from one direction to another as if they had a mind of their own.

"Oh, my God," one of the officers said in a hushed whisper, as the building started to emit a soft glow.

With a force that made the earth all around them shake, all sides of the building crumpled inward almost in unison, as if someone had crumpled it up like a ball of paper.

There were screams and hollers as officers tried desperately to shield themselves from the ensuing dust cloud it spat out in its wake. A few cars in front were hit, causing them to erupt in a blaze of fire.

Tim stopped his car and got out, shielding his eyes against the heat and dust. When it stopped, the once majestic building was nothing but rubble. He stared at it for a moment. "Damn. Too late."

Inside Tim's car, Cathy fell into Mike's arms, crying uncontrollably. He put his arms around her, as he looked in hatred at the smouldering pile of rubble. Then his expression changed. He smiled. "Everyone... Look!"

A board fell over in the debris, revealing a small pocket created by the blast. Xander Drew stepped out of it. He was covered in soot, bleeding from every crevice in his body, torn both physically and mentally, limping, shocked beyond human comprehension and overall looked like grim death. It was Xander, just the same.

"Xander!" Cathy cried, getting out of the car and running toward him with Mike not far behind. They embraced him, tears of joy streaming down all three faces. They fell to the ground, kneeling on the wet soil, still embraced.

Xander leaned in and kissed Cathy on the forehead. "It's alright."

Suddenly, there was more movement from the tattered building, a loud crash.

"I'll KILL you for this!" Genblade screamed as he burst from the smelting pile of rubble. He pointed his sword at Xander and was about to throw it directly at his head, when...

-click- -click - click- click -click- -click - click-

Fifty handguns trained themselves on Genblade at once. Red laser sights dotted along Genblade's forehead and chest. The killer's eyes moved through the crowd, searching out Tim White. He found him, found the hatred in the policeman's eyes. He continued looking through the crowd, and found what he was looking for. Xander got up from the warm embrace that he, Cathy, and Mike had been sharing. He stood straight and rigid, glaring at his back at his enemy. Genblade's sneer moved slowly into a smile as he mouthed the words:

'It'll never be over.'

Xander didn't flinch.

Genblade seemed to love it. He released his grip on the double -sided blade. It fell to the ground with a final

-clink-

Genblade smiled at Xander once more as he put his hands above his head.

EPILOGUE

"Let us pray," Reverend Robert Gallagher said, over-looking the coffin.

Xander would have loved for it to be an open casket, to be able to say goodbye to her one last time, but the damage Genblade did was so extensive they had to leave it closed. The emotion of the situation nearly made the Black Womb surface, but he held it in.

The priest continued, "Lord, we gather to lay to rest your daughter, Sara. We ask that you welcome her into your heavenly kingdom and give repose to her soul. Through Christ, our lord, Amen."

I've been up all night trying to write... something *that could express what I'm feeling. Every time I tried, it kept coming out like a confession instead of a eulogy. But how can I possibly do Sara justice with just a few pages of scribbles soaked with a flood of tears? What can I say to these people to even remotely portray to them what Sara was and how much she meant to me?*

"I've asked Alexander Drew, Sara's long time friend, to say a few words about the young woman we all held such a special place in our hearts for. Mister Drew?"

It's vulgar - playing the role of the helpless boy. I caused her death.

I feel like the worst kind of liar.

Xander got up from his seat in the second row and started toward the pulpit, a piece of paper shaking uncontrollably in his hands. He walked over to Reverend Gallagher, who put an assuring hand on his shoulder before stepping aside. The simple empathetic contact sent shivers throughout his body. Deep down inside him, the womb organ twitched once, as if to shake back.

"Hello," he started, "this may take a while." He cleared his throat, staring out into the crowd. It was filled with friends, family, classmates, relatives... "Ahem. Um... Sara was..."

He stopped.

"Sara was..."

He looked up from his paper, tears streaming down his face. *No. There are no words.* He walked over to the coffin and placed his hand upon its white surface. It felt cold and inhuman, but he still felt her in it. As if she were connected to it in some way. "I'll miss you."

There are no words.

Then he left the church with tears in his eyes.

As soon as Xander stepped through the door into the cool night air, the Womb overpowered him, black ooze flowing over him.

I'll never live it down. Sara's death can never be justified. But this I know: I'm going to spend the rest of my life making up for it.

A few blocks away, a mugger clubbed a young girl over the head, smiling as he rolled up his sleeves, revealing a red letter 'T' tattooed on his right arm. "...come 'ere, sweet thing..."

Genblade plead guilty to all the murders, even the ones that I committed. I guess his sense of honor realized that I beat him and that I should get something for it.

"... no.... please, stop."

I'll never stop, Sara. I'll keep my promise, protect the innocent from the scum. All the scum. Be it big like Alpha or small like Grendel. They're all guilty.

"... please... just stop."

If you're innocent...

"...stop..."

You're hurt...

"...please..."

Or you're scared...

A black figure dropped from the sky and kicked the mugger in the face, sending him sprawling to the ground.

I'll be there.

PREVIEW

TRANSFORMATIONS IN PAIN

SHE RAN

She turned the corner quickly, scraping her shoulder against the brick.

Her breath came in quick, labored pants as her feet slammed against the pavement one after the other, displacing mounds of gravel and mud as she went. It had rained the night before, and the asphalt was slick and wet beneath the soles of her feet. Fighting to maintain her balance, she turned around to see how far she had gone. Her auburn hair caught on her eyelashes as it whipped around her head, making it hard to see.

They were still back there. She couldn't see them now, but she could hear them. Could hear their puffs of breath and their own footfalls, as well as the steady stream of curses that one of them kept up in constant supply between bouts of a hacking smoker's cough. The other one was stronger, his legs pumping like pistons. The sounds of his heels slamming against the street were louder than the other one. He was closer, but it was hard to tell exactly how close because he remained deathly silent as he advanced upon her.

It had started about three blocks back. Every time she

had stopped, they had stopped. Every time she sped up, they sped up. She hadn't been sure what to think at first, then she'd seen the knife sticking out of one of their belts, only partially obscured by his red-and-gold sport jacket. Her eyes had lit up and felt twice their normal size. For a moment it had been all she could do to stare at it, glimmering against the faded denim.

She turned away fast, pushing some hair out of her face to try and hide the fear in her eyes and make her exit seem casual. Whether or not they had been fooled they still followed, keeping roughly ten meters between themselves and the girl at all times.

She turned down Laird Street, the way she always did on her way home from school, then dropped her knapsack and broke into a run. When her two pursuers turned the corner a few seconds behind her they found that their ten meter buffer had become closer to thirty, and took off running after her.

Her chest heaved fire now, her stomach clenching in continuous bursts of agony as she cursed the potato chips she'd had for lunch. She could feel their jagged little edges digging into the lining of her gut, tearing at her from the inside out as her abdomen contracted with each step she forced out of her body.

She'd spent the latter part of her last semester skipping Phys Ed class in favor of hanging out with the boys in the smoking section or text-messaging her cousin. Anything to not have to be covered in sweat for the rest of the day, in a school where the air conditioners seemed to be mostly for decoration.

As a stitch developed in her lower left side and her

legs began to feel numb and rubbery, she began to wish that she had been a little more health conscious.

She felt blood trickle down her arm from where she'd scraped it. She bit her lip as she pumped her arms and focused all her attention on the street corner just one building length away from her. After that, she would be on her street. Not long after that, she'd be home. She'd be safe.

She heard a loud curse close behind her, but dared not turn around to see. It was the one word she'd never say herself, even in the worst of situations, and just the sound of it curdled in her ears until it was almost all she could hear.

She tried not to think about it as she closed her eyes tight and poured on the steam, willing her legs to pump harder and faster than they ever had before. She didn't know what they wanted with her, but she knew she didn't want to find out anytime soon. She heard something in her knee pop like when her Biology teacher cracked his knuckles. Fresh pain shot up her leg and into her spine, burying in deep and making a home there.

When she opened her eyes again, she was almost at the curb. She could see her next-door neighbor's house, dissected by the wall she was about to pass. The windows were dark and the blinds were closed tight, their usually inviting porch now looking cold and desolate. Someone had taken all of the flowers inside and she realized, strangely, that they were on vacation. She didn't know why that occurred to her at that moment, only that it did.

Behind her, one of the footsteps stopped and was replaced by very loud breathing and panting. Without even turning around, she could see the thinner of her two pursuers hunched over with his hands against his knees. He was trying to catch his breath, sweat getting caught in his short brown hair. The other set of footsteps just got louder and faster, as if he had only been moving at that speed so that his friend could keep up. If they were any indication, he'd be on her in seconds.

She turned the corner, ready to dart across the road and into her driveway faster than she ever had before, hoping that there were no cars coming. Instead her nose crashed into something hard and she fell backward. Her backbone slammed against the pavement. She felt her entire body quake with the sudden impact, aching from the base of her skull right down to her ankles.

The man she had bumped into also fell to the ground and looked to have skidded out his elbow in the process.

Stunned, she wasn't fully aware of the passage of time until she felt two massive hands clamp down on her shoulders like vice grips. They brought her to her feet.

"Get the car," the man behind her said with a high-pitched voice. It was not the man that was holding her -- he was the one that had lost his breath. By the sounds of things, he still had yet to regain it.

The lanky man in front of her smirked as he rose to his feet. Then turned and looked over his shoulder at the row of houses behind him.

"No!" she screamed as the man who held her pulled her close. He forced her to walk with him toward the nearby alley. She tried to hit and kick at her capture, but it seemed to have as much effect as hitting solid stone. She continued to scream even after they dragged her away. Eventually the screaming stopped, long before her terror was over.

It occurred to her that nothing would ever be the same again. Someone had told her once that every time that happens in life, it was like a caterpillar changing into a butterfly. A transition and transformation into something different.

This time, she thought, it was a transformation... in pain.

AFTERWORD

This book started a long relationship between myself and the character of Xander Drew. I didn't know him as well when I wrote this as I do now, but he remains a constant in my life.

Some of my views have changed since penning this book, particularly my feelings on violence, a theme that runs through this series. I have resisted the urge to back-edit these texts and instead implore readers to consider the series to now be functionally about these changes in the portrayal of violence going forward. I feel like denying that we once thought of things differently denies our personal growth.

I'd like to thank my editor Erin Vance for all her help on this text.

This book is dedicated to my partner, Ellen Curtis, who makes me a better writer. Every day.

Matthew LeDrew
February 15, 2019
St. Johns, Newfoundland

ENGEN TIMELINE

With over twenty novels spread over three different series by many different authors, the Engen Universe of titles is growing every day and into genres we couldn't have imagined! From the original ten book *Coral Beach Casefiles* thriller series, its crime novel sequel series *Xander Drew*, our flagship adventure title *Infinity*, or single-novels like *Jacobi Street* or *light⎮dark*, there's something in the Engen Universe for everyone with more books by more authors on the way soon!

...But how do the events relate to one another, chronologically? While some astute readers have guessed at the potential timeline (some accurately, some not), we're going to finally set the question of the Engen Timeline to rest.

Turn the page for an up-to-date guide of the ever-widening world of Engen, featuring the works of Ellen Curtis, Andrea Hackett, Sarah Thompson, Jay Paulin, and Matthew LeDrew!

In the 10 Years Prior Black September

"Reptilia" by Matthew LeDrew
published in *light l dark*.
Danger descends on a small secluded town in the form of a deadly virus with fantastic and terrible side-effects. Can a small group of doctors escape alive?

Compendium by Ellen Curtis
Three short stories forming the basis for the Engen Universe's ties to suspense, genetic engeneering, and the supernatural. Features the stories "The Tourniquet Revival," "Falling into Fire" and "At Midnight, the Dawn."

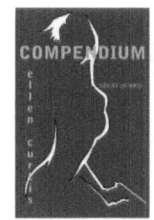

"The Theogony" by Matthew LeDrew
published in *light l dark*.
A tale of young Theo Flaherty of the *Infinity* series and his time admitted against his will to the Black Springs hospital, where he learns to paint, and seeks out his father.

Black September

"Revving Engen" by Matthew LeDrew
published in *light l dark*.
A direct lead-in to both *Infinity* and *Black Womb*, Tasha travels to Coral Beach, Maine on a hot tip about a recently discovered young man with incredible abilities.

Infinity by Ellen Curtis & Matthew LeDrew
Faced with a destiny he's uncertain of, the enigmatic Victor must bring together four unique people with very special abilities… or face the tasks ahead alone. Guaranteed to excite!

Black Womb by Matthew LeDrew
Fifteen years ago, something happened in Coral Beach, Maine that resulted in the present death of a seventeen-year-old boy. Now four high-school students must try to solve the mystery… before the killer picks them off.

Jacobi Street by Matthew LeDrew
When a mysterious painting shows up at an art gallery he works at, Bob must work with Eddie and Sloan to track down its sinister origins and convince the people living on Jacobi Street of them, before its too late!

Transformations in Pain by Matthew LeDrew
When two girls are assaulted and one is hospitalized, the residents of Coral Beach must put their shared tragedies behind them and stop the man responsible, as well as unlock the secrets behind the true nature of the Womb…

Year One: October

Smoke and Mirrors by Matthew LeDrew
The approaching trial of Genblade brings closure to the people of Coral Beach, until people start showing up dead in the same manner they did when he was at large.

"Scarlett" by Andrea Hackett
published in *light | dark*.
Introducing Scarlett, the slightly damaged hunter on a mission to save others from the monsters from her past.

"The Inevitable" by Ali House
published in *The Lightbulb Forest*
A young woman must contend with the
emergence of a frightening new power alongside
the emotional high of a first date.

The Tourniquet Reprisal by Curtis & LeDrew
A man lives in Atlanta, Georgia that people
don't talk about, but everyone knows he's there.
He arrived a year ago and turned a gaggle
of uneducated youth into something new,
something to fear.

Roulette by Matthew LeDrew
As the teen suicide rate in Coral Beach starts to
climb astronomically fast, Xander travels to Los
Angeles to fight his most terrifying adversary
yet… and learns that the only thing worse than
looking for release… is finding it.

Year One: November

Exodus of Angels by Curtis & LeDrew
Victor's enigmatic past is illuminated when
Jaycee accompanies him to visit a new friend
in the paliative care ward of the Black Springs
hospital, where Theo also happens to be
searching for a cure for Leigh.

Ghosts of the Past by Matthew LeDrew
Coral Beach faces its most awesome threat when
one of Engen's past mistakes is unleashed upon
the unsuspecting populous. Friends and enemies
unite to fight a common enemy… but will even
that be enough?

Touch Your Nose by Matthew LeDrew
Simon Monk must infiltrate the San Fransico
branch of Shane Industries, a massive company
with deep ties to the Engen Universe. Where do
his true loyalties lie? And can he get out without
causing harm?

Ignorance is Bliss by Matthew LeDrew
After being set through the ringer one too many
times, Xander decides that his life with Julie
needs a little more attention… which is bad news
because a new villain has come to town with his
sights set on Adam Genblade.

"Gristle While You Work" by Jay Paulin
published in *light | dark*.
A short story centering around the rise of a new,
and possibly cannibalistic, serial killer in the
Engen Universe.

Becoming by Matthew LeDrew
For months Xander Drew has been doing his
level best to keep the streets of Coral Beach clean,
which means it's time for the forces of darkness to
strike back… all at once.

Inner Child by Matthew LeDrew
Julie is hospitalized with life-threatening wounds
to both body and soul. But the real threat comes
from the hospital walls themselves, as a demonic
presence makes itself known to Xander and his
friends.

End of Year One

Gang War by Matthew LeDrew
The Tees, a homicidal gang of evil men, has finally been taken down by Xander Drew. But his victory is short lived, as retired Tees are mysteriously killed. With a town of suspects, anyone can be the culprit… including one of their own.

Chains by Matthew LeDrew
Sociopath Derek Smith has been freed from prison and is praying on the weak; and none are weaker than August Styles: a pregnant girl with Down Syndrome who has run away from home.

"Omega" by Ellen Curtis
published in *light | dark*.
A sinister division of Engen begins a series of experiments on pregnant women in a fashion eerily similar to those that created the original Black Womb project.

The Long Road by Matthew LeDrew
Xander meets the American people — and realizes that the world is harsh and wicked, but can also be soft and gentle, even loving. Xander Drew comes of age on the road, and sets his new direction.

Year Two

Cinders by Matthew LeDrew
Detective Horton enters a violent and dangerous world he didn't know existed beneath the veneer of order and structure that he has based his entire deductive method around.

Sinister Intent by Matthew LeDrew
One of the killers Detective Horton could not catch has resurfaced: a serial killer who flaunts his sinister intent in front of the Los Angeles Police Department, making it so that no one is safe.

Faith by Matthew LeDrew
Xander's mysterious and troublesome past returns to haunt him on the streets of Los Angeles; a place where even more people can get caught in the crossfire of the games of death and deceit that makes up his life.

Flickers in the Night by Matthew LeDrew
Lisa Rowdan is hunted by her haunting -- and powerful -- ex-boyfriend Ryan through a lonely city street. Can she escape him?
One of over twenty great sprine-tingling short stories!

Family Values by Matthew LeDrew
Xander and his new friends Crowley, Lisa, and Tim investigate a series of kidnappings and murders that stretch back decades, all of which have the same similar twist: victims being found after years of being missing.

The Future

Fate's Shadow by Matthew LeDrew
When one of Xander's old cases comes up for trial, Megan Greene returns with it. The former friends are led into conflict regarding her client's innocence. However, they put their difference aside when they both become targets of the vigilante known as Shiro Gilbert.

The Future

"Remers" by Sarah Thompson
published in *light | dark*.
In the not-too-distant future of the Engen
Universe, young athletes are the targets of a
scouting program to create the next stage of super
soldier with cybernetic enhancements.

The early years of **Xander Drew** as he struggles with the evils of his small rural hometown of Coral Beach, Maine. Cursed with the heart of the Womb and the gift of seeing the world around him for what it really is, Xander must learn the hard lessons about the nature of humanity to traverse the minefield of criminals, gangs, and abusers that stand between him and ultimate happiness -- but most of all that **sometimes it takes a monster, to catch a monster.**

"THE WRITING OF ITS GENERATION-- VISUAL, TO-THE-POINT AND IN-THE-MOMENT."
- *The Northeast Avalon Times*

The Coral Beach Casefiles series by Matthew LeDrew:

Book One: Black Womb (February 2019)
Book Two: Transformations in Pain (March 2019)
Book Three: Smoke and Mirrors (April 2019)
Book Four: Roulette (May 2019)
Book Five: Ghosts of the Past (June 2019)
Book Six: Ignorance is Bliss (July 2019)
Book Seven: Becoming (August 2019)
Book Eight: Inner Child (September 2019)
Book Nine: Gang War (October 2019)
Book Ten: Chains (November 2019)

Epilogue: The Long Road (December 2019)

For more information, please visit

www.engenbooks.com

THE XANDER DREW SERIES

Prologue: The Long Road (December 2019)

Book One: Cinders (April 2015)
Book Two: Sinister Intent (November 2015)
Book Thee: Faith (December 2017)
Book Four: Family Values (December 2018)
Book Five: Fate's Shadow (forthcoming)

COMING SOON FROM ENGEN BOOKS:

FATE'S SHADOW

A violent past case is reopened as Xander must contend with
Detective Thomas Horton, the vigilante Shadow Flame, and
a returning figure from his youth in Coral Beach -- all while
trying to prevent a murderer from running free. Can Xander
stay the course even as his world crashes in around him?

infinity

The world is changing, and we have to change with it. That was the one thing that Victor was really sure of when he started looking for special people: people who could change the possibilities of the future from something certainly grim... to something *infinitely* positive.

Now four unsuspecting people from different backgrounds and walks of life have been thrown into the mix together, and nothing will ever be the same. But there's a difference between hoping for a better world and actually having one, and there will always be resistance to change.

Book One: Infinity (October 2010)
Book Two: The Tourniquet Reprisal (October 2012)
Book Three: Exodus of Angels (April 2016)

Related Books:
        Compendium (October 2009)
        light|dark (April 2012)
        Roulette (October 2009)
        The Long Road (May 2014)

Written by the superstar author team of Ellen Curtis (*Compendium*) and Matthew LeDrew (the *Xander Drew* series).

Destiny doesn't wait for anyone.

ABOUT THE
AUTHOR

Matthew LeDrew holds an Honours Degree in English from the Memorial University of Newfoundland with a minor in Anthropology, and studied Journalism at College of the North Atlantic in Stephenville, Newfoundland. He was honoured to be a jury member of the 2018 NLBA awards.

He has written twenty novels for Engen Books: the ten book *Coral Beach Casefiles* series, *The Long Road*, *Cinders*, *Sinister Intent*, *Faith*, *Family Values*, *Jacobi Street*, *Touch Your Nose*, *Infinity*, *The Tourniquet Reprisal*, and *Exodus of Angels* the latter three of which with co-author Ellen Curtis.

He lives in St. Johns, Newfoundland.